You nev

girlfriend is going to stop by and
shoot you....

"I need to find my son."

Katie studied the cabin. She knew in her heart she was staring at the one man who could get the job done, lead her into the mountains and rescue Tyler. Her gaze lingered for a second on the bed as she wondered what it would be like to lie beside a hero instead of a criminal.

"You've got to help me find him. He's got my son and I need him back. You don't know what Lee's capable of."

Gray knew how utterly dangerous a woman could be, worse than shrapnel if she got too close. If only he could close the door on his past and the hold she had over him.

He took a step, anger flashing in his eyes. "I'm not available."

He'd left her no choice. Suddenly, Katie was aiming a .22 pistol at him.

Dear Reader,

Ever since I was a little girl I've been fascinated with the mountains. My mom, a figure skating judge, used to take me to competitions in places like Colorado Springs where I saw the Rockies for the first time. I was hooked!

As a writer of romantic suspense, I love setting my books in interesting places. Gray and Katie's story in *Soldier Surrender* unfolds in the Cascade Mountains of Washington, and my April 2008 Harlequin Intrigue is set in the Colorado Rockies.

After spending forty years in the Midwest, I moved to the Pacific Northwest where, on a clear day, I can see the Cascade and Olympic mountain ranges and even Mt. Rainier. I feel fortunate, indeed.

For me, the mountains offer peace and adventure. I hope you enjoy this adventure about childhood friends who come to terms with their past and fall in love.

Your mountain-loving friend,

Pat White

PAT WHITE

SOLDIER SURRENDER

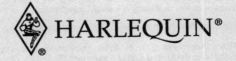

TORONTO • NEW YORK • LONDON
AMSTERDAM • PARIS • SYDNEY • HAMBURG
STOCKHOLM • ATHENS • TOKYO • MILAN • MADRID
PRAGUE • WARSAW • BUDAPEST • AUCKLAND

To Shirley Sherman for sharing her love of
the mountains with me.

ISBN-13: 978-0-373-69305-4
ISBN-10:   0-373-69305-2

SOLDIER SURRENDER

www.eHarlequin.com

Printed in U.S.A.

ABOUT THE AUTHOR

Pat White has been spinning stories in her head ever since she was a little girl growing up in the Midwest, stories filled with mystery, romance and adventure. Years later, while trying to solve the mysteries of raising a family in a house full of men, she started writing romantic fiction. After six Golden Heart Award nominations and a *Romantic Times BOOKreviews* Award for Best Contemporary Romance (2004), her passion for storytelling and love of a good romance continue to find a voice in her tales of romantic suspense. Pat now lives in the Pacific Northwest, and she's still trying to solve the mysteries of living in a house full of men—with the added complication of two silly dogs and three spoiled cats. She loves to hear from readers, so please visit her at www.patwhitebooks.com.

Books by Pat White

HARLEQUIN INTRIGUE

*The Blackwell Group

CAST OF CHARACTERS

Adam "Gray" Turner—A former Special Ops agent turned mountain recluse, Gray hides from buried shame until his high school crush shows up on his doorstep demanding his help.

Katie Meyers Anderson—A devoted mother, Katie is desperate to find her son Tyler, who's been taken into the rugged Cascade Mountains by her criminal ex-husband.

Lee Anderson—Katie's drug-dealing ex is out to punish her for turning him in to authorities.

Federal agent Sam Washburn—Although he offers Katie a deal if she gets him evidence against her ex-husband, Washburn suspects she's an accomplice in Lee's drug business.

Jacob Robinson—A local tracker who's dragged into the middle of this domestic dispute.

Deputy Tom Connor—The local law enforcement officer believes if anyone can make sense of this mess, military hero Gray Turner can.

Hoot—Gray's childhood mentor, Hoot, died of a heart attack after having been brought in for questioning by police. Gray blames himself for his friend's death. If Gray hadn't been trying to protect Katie, Hoot might still be alive today.

Chapter One

Gray Turner had just returned from a relaxing trail ride in the Cascade Mountains when he sensed an intruder on his property.

He hesitated as he brushed down Maverick in the barn. Could be his imagination.

Squirt's crazed barking echoed from the cabin a hundred yards away, confirming Gray's suspicions. He tossed the brush aside, slid the Glock from its holster and readied himself for whatever waited outside the barn door.

Not many folks would risk trespassing on his land. The locals of Millsworth, Washington, knew he didn't welcome surprise guests. Or any guests for that matter.

He clicked into defensive mode as adrenaline blocked out all sound but the Border collie's warning.

Gray had to be overreacting. He wasn't in

combat anymore. He'd left Special Ops three years ago, settling in this remote spot. Sure, he'd done some freelance work, but he'd never revealed his location to business associates.

The brisk mountain air whistled through the rafters. Squirt's barking grew more frantic. Maybe the guy was after whatever he could steal from the cabin. He'd be disappointed as hell.

Gray calmed his breathing, as he had so many times before an assault, and peered through the wooden slats. A mysterious figure stepped onto his front porch. Didn't the perp have the good sense to back off when the dog started barking?

Using the trees as cover, Gray made his silent approach. The intruder went to the front window and peered inside the cabin. Bold bastard.

Bold and small, judging from where the top of his head hit the window. Squirt pounded on the glass like a good watchdog.

Figuring his visitor was distracted by the dog, Gray took a few steps closer. The unwelcome guest placed his hand to the glass.

A very petite-looking hand. Damn, it was a woman.

Still, Gray knew how utterly dangerous a woman could be, worse than shrapnel if she got too close.

He holstered the Glock and crept up the opposite side of the porch. He didn't care if she was a woman, man or a friggin' army general. She was trespassing.

Gray stepped up behind her. "Who the hell are you?"

She screamed and spun around, swinging her shoulder bag.

"Damn it, woman!" He grabbed her wrist and she lunged to bite him. He spun her around and applied an arm lock to neutralize her.

"Stop, help, police!" she cried.

"Police? Why do you want the police? So they can arrest you for trespassing?" he said against her ear. He noticed her hair was dirty blond with streaks of sunlight.

"Stop, I said stop!" she demanded.

"Calm down. I'm not going to hurt you."

"You *are* hurting me."

"Then stop squirming."

She did, but he sensed she wouldn't stay calm for long.

"What are you doing on my property?" he said. Damn if her hair didn't smell of fresh wildflowers. It had been too long since he'd had a woman in his bed. Maybe it was time for a trip to the city for a night of mindless sex.

"I came to see Adam Turner," she said.

Adam? No one had called him Adam since high school.

"Why?" he questioned.

"I need his help."

He released her and she took a few steps away. When she turned to face him, she clutched her shoulder bag like a shield.

"What do you want?" he said.

"Adam? Don't you remember me? It's Katie Meyers."

The wind ripped from his chest as he struggled to make sense of it. Katie Meyers. His first love. His first heartbreak.

The girl who caused him to lose his honor.

"Katie?" he whispered. He studied the once bright-faced, sweet-looking girl who'd lured him with her innocent smiles and tender voice. She looked much older even though it had been only eleven years. Faint worry lines creased her forehead; weariness dimmed her green eyes.

Not his problem.

"I know I have no right to ask—"

"Then don't," he interrupted. "How the hell did you find me?"

"Luke Dunham came back to Redmond after being discharged and told me where you were."

His special ops buddy, Dunham, had given Gray up to this…this what? She was nothing to him but a childhood mistake.

"Luke said you lived out here and I remembered how good you were at tracking, when you…" she hesitated "…were a kid."

When you hung out with Hoot, that's what she was about to say. That was a lifetime ago, and Gray had worked hard to forget the past.

To forget that Hoot was dead, thanks to Gray.

"Adam, I need to find my son."

She had a child with another man. Something twisted in his gut. Good God, you're still fantasizing about the girl who stripped you of your dignity over ten years ago?

"Call the police," Gray said.

"I…I can't."

"Why the hell not?"

"It's complicated."

Gray narrowed his eyes. "Hold on, are you running from the law?"

"Of course not."

"Then call the cops."

"They won't take me seriously. Tyler is with his father."

He put out his hands. "I'm not getting involved in a domestic issue. I'm not a cop or a shrink."

He opened the cabin door, commanding Squirt to back off.

"But they said you're a hero."

Her words cut him like a switchblade. Heroes don't betray friends, or run from their past.

"I'm no hero." He turned. "Just a man who wants to be left alone."

"Adam, please."

Those damned green eyes lured him in again, taunted him with the promise of love and tenderness that he knew didn't exist for dishonorable bastards like Gray Turner.

She shivered against a cool burst of wind, wrapping her red scarf tighter around her neck. Red, a fitting color. A warning sign of danger ahead.

"I've got names of guides who can help you for a price," he said. "I'm not one of them."

Following him inside she said, "I remember you being a lot nicer when we were kids."

"I don't remember being a kid."

KATIE TOOK A MOMENT TO stroke the Border collie's neck.

"Squirt, come," Adam ordered.

The dog raced to his master's side. Adam didn't look up, but rather focused on making coffee in the kitchenette. He'd kept his distance since they'd come inside.

A good thing considering he seemed nothing like the sweet kid she knew growing up. She couldn't get used to how much he'd changed, how his shoulders seemed broader, his eyes darker...and his smile nonexistent.

Katie rubbed her hands together to warm them, and studied the one-room cabin. A kitchenette consisted of a wooden table for two. An overstuffed chair and sturdy rocker faced the fireplace in the main living area, and a queen bed covered with a dark green plaid blanket filled the corner of the cabin. Her gaze lingered for a second as she imagined this man sprawled beneath the sheets. She wondered what it would be like to lie beside a hero instead of a criminal.

Why had she stayed with Lee so long? Because she'd ached for her marriage to work, even after she'd found out about his business. Silly girl, she'd thought she could talk him out of being a drug dealer.

That's when she'd discovered how charming and manipulative he was. He'd promised, but had never intended to quit, so she demanded a divorce.

Yet here she was: the cops suspected Katie of being involved in his business, and her son had been taken by her monster ex-husband.

No one was concerned about Tyler because they didn't believe he was in danger.

So, she'd had no choice.

Find out how he gets the drugs out of the country and I'll make sure you and your son are safe, FBI Agent Washburn had offered.

Maybe she should have worked with the Feds sooner, but she couldn't stand the thought of spending time with Lee to uncover his plans, especially after…

Can't think about that now. Focus on finding Tyler.

She'd never felt safe in her childhood home thanks to Dad's drunken rages and Mom's ambivalence. She'd promised herself that her child would not live that way, which was why she'd been drawn to the "perfect" Lee Anderson.

"Here." Adam handed her a chipped ceramic mug. Squirt stayed close to his master.

She took the mug and their fingers touched. Something sparked in his eyes and he turned away. He *was* still attracted to her. She sipped her coffee, a plan forming in her mind. Maybe she could convince him to help after all.

Yet there was something threatening about the adult Adam Turner. He hummed with an intensity she'd never sensed as a kid. The young Adam Turner had been gentle and tender.

Safe.

As her friend Luke Dunham had warned, war changes a man.

Or had it started years ago when Gray's father figure, Hoot, had died? She inhaled the scent of strong coffee, fighting back the guilt. She'd been partially responsible for that. The things you did for the people you loved. She opened her eyes and watched Gray settle in the rocker across the room.

"I'm surprised a guy like you lives all alone in this gorgeous part of the world," she began.

He eyed her and sipped his coffee.

Suddenly she wished she'd taken more time with

her makeup this morning. But she didn't think she'd be seducing a stranger.

"Who did you end up marrying?" Adam asked.

"Lee Anderson."

He snorted in disapproval, the sound setting off self-condemnation all over again. She shoved it back.

"Yeah, I was young and naive," she admitted.

Truth was, Lee had been a decent husband in the beginning. Then he lost his job and their perfect life crumbled. He announced he was going to work for himself, selling a specialty line of chocolate.

She had believed the lie.

She'd believed a lot of things, like his promise never to hurt her. The black memory flooded her thoughts. Lee grabbing her, shoving her against the wall…

Tyler playing video games in the next room.

She took a sip of bitter coffee to shock her back to the present. *Move on, get your son back and start a new life where Lee can never find you.*

"I was an idealistic girl," she said, ambling over to Adam and setting her coffee cup on the end table. "But I'm a grown woman now."

Terrified to make her next move, she was driven by the image of Tyler shivering in a cold, dark tent, crying for his mom.

She reached out and touched Adam's cheek. "I've missed you, Adam." It wasn't a complete lie.

She had missed his compassion and his gentle nature.

He stood, breaking contact, and brushed past her to the fireplace. "The name is Gray. No one calls me Adam anymore."

"Sorry, Gray." She took a deep breath and tried again. His attraction was obvious. If she could only mask her desperation and do this right.

She started toward him. "You've grown up to be a true American hero."

"Hardly." He studied the burning wood in the fireplace.

"It doesn't surprise me," she continued. "You were always so clever growing up, smarter than the rest of the guys."

She'd been fascinated by him back then, by his ability to build a fort in the woods and track animals with such ease. Most of the boys her age were into drinking and girls. Adam was gentle and inquisitive. Even though she'd wanted to belong to the popular group—Lee's group—a part of her felt more comfortable around Adam Turner.

"I heard you led dangerous missions."

"I followed orders."

His curt response made her wonder why he chose not to brag about his accomplishments.

"You did more than follow orders. You saved lives." She stepped in front of him, blocking his view of the fire. With her forefinger and thumb she turned his face to look at her.

She hesitated at the intensity of his blue eyes. Could she really do this?

Tyler, think of Tyler.

"I always had a thing for you," she confessed.

"What are you talking about?"

She slid her hand up his neck into his thick, brown hair. "You felt it, too, didn't you?"

"I don't feel anything."

The need in his eyes spoke otherwise. He *did* still want her. She'd sensed his crush when they were teenagers, but Adam Turner had been quiet. He wasn't popular or sophisticated. He wasn't the football star. She'd wanted so desperately to land the perfect guy, a hero who would give her love and security.

She'd wanted it so badly she'd created a mirage.

"I've often wondered what kind of man you'd become." With her hand to the back of his head, she coaxed his lips to hers.

Closer.

His lips were full and wanting. She felt his hands grip her upper arms. She inhaled his scent of worn leather mixed with pine.

Closer.

Kissing him, seducing him, was the only option left.

The warmth of his breath caressed her face. She

should feel ashamed and dirty for the seduction, but all she could think about was her son's tearstained cheeks.

Adam's lips touched hers and a bubble of emotion clogged her throat. This was the first time she'd felt a true connection to anyone in years. She'd distanced herself from Lee, from her judgmental father and from her friends.

Parting her lips, she invited him to deepen the kiss. She didn't expect his moan of surrender. Guilt tore through her chest.

Adam slid his arm to her lower back to pull her close. For a second this felt real, like a lover's embrace. She'd often wondered if she'd feel comfortable letting a man touch her again.

This wasn't any man. Adam was the man who could find her son.

His need pressed against her and she reached between them, brushing her hand against his jeans.

He wrenched away, hands gripping her shoulders. "What the hell are you doing?"

She felt naked. Ashamed.

She regained her composure. "Isn't this what you want?"

He released her as if he'd been shocked by a thousand volts of electricity. "You manipulative little—"

"Adam, listen—"

"You haven't changed much." He went to the

kitchenette, splayed his hands across the breakfast bar and stared her down. "Still using your charms to get what you want?"

This wasn't going to work.

"I need you," she said, her voice sounding cold and indifferent, even to her. "I have money."

He jerked upright as if he'd been slapped. He still wanted the innocent, sweet Katie—a girl who no longer existed.

She reached into her purse, careful not to expose the pink-lady pistol that guaranteed she'd never be helpless again.

"You are one cold bitch," he said.

Her hand froze as it clamped around the wallet stuffed with hundreds. That had to be enough, right? Enough to tempt even a recluse like Adam to help her?

Obviously her seduction hadn't.

You are one cold bitch.

More like a desperate mother. She went to him, ignoring his fierce expression, and slapped the bills on the counter. "Two thousand."

"I don't want your money," he said with disgust, and went to the fireplace. Obviously he couldn't stand to be near her.

But she needed Adam, not some ordinary tracker. She'd heard he was a ruthless warrior who won battles using his keen instinct and survival skill.

"Adam…" she began.

He glared at her.

"I'm sorry. Gray. Luke said you're the best and you know this land better than anyone."

"Not true. I'll get you names of three guys who are competent trackers."

He went to the kitchen, opened a drawer and pulled out a pad of paper and address book. He scribbled a few names and numbers, ripped a sheet from the pad and handed it to her. "Jacob Robinson would be my number one pick," he said as if they hadn't kissed, as if she hadn't touched him.

What had she done?

"If he's unavailable, try Clovis Smith or Trey Edwards."

"I don't want them. I want you."

He took a step toward her, anger flashing in his eyes. "*I'm* not available."

Her breath caught. She'd been in control a few minutes ago when she'd made her advances, but now she felt like a trapped fawn at the hunter's mercy.

"What's happened to you?" she whispered.

Ripping his gaze from hers, he marched to the window. He fingered the sheer curtain aside and squinted into the darkness. "Damn, more company."

His distaste for visitors was obvious.

Tough. She needed his skill and knowledge of the surrounding mountains to find her son, to finally end this.

Gray opened the cabin door. "Deputy Connor?"

She heard a man step onto the porch. "A pretty-looking female came looking for you a few hours ago."

Gray motioned toward Katie.

The cop peeked inside. Even the cops were afraid to enter Gray's cabin without a formal invitation.

"Ma'am, glad to see you found your friend," the deputy said.

She noticed Gray clench his jaw at the use of the word *friend.* Her heart sank. This man was never going to help her no matter who was at risk or how much money she offered.

Panic settled low in her chest. If Lee took their son across the border into Canada, how would she find him?

"Coffee?" Gray offered the deputy.

"Actually, I'd like a word outside. Sorry to interrupt, miss."

"No, it's fine."

"Squirt, stay," Gray ordered, then closed the door on Katie.

IF ONLY GRAY COULD CLOSE the door on his past and the hold she had over him. He'd lost his senses when she'd kissed him, touched him. But she wasn't kissing him because she cared about him.

She wanted something.

Didn't matter. He wouldn't be suckered in again.

It was bad enough she'd persuaded him to keep quiet when they were teenagers.

Deputy Connor led Gray away from the cabin to the patrol car.

"What's up, Tom?"

They'd shared a beer now and then. Gray was a celebrity of sorts with local law enforcement.

Tom leaned against his squad car. "How well do you know Katie Anderson?"

"We grew up together."

"When was the last time you spoke with her?"

Hard to forget that day. "More than a decade ago."

"And nothing since then?"

"No, why?" This seemed more serious than the local law checking out a stranger.

"Did a little digging after she stopped by the station. Her ex-husband is an ex-con. Served three years for a drug charge. They suspected the wife was involved but couldn't prove it."

Hell, Katie Meyers was a drug dealer?

"Arrest her," Gray demanded.

"For what?"

"Trespassing on my property."

"Looks to me like you invited her in for coffee."

Gray rolled his neck. He liked simple things: a one-room cabin, one horse, one dog and no females to complicate his life.

Especially this female.

"Why the visit after all these years?" Tom asked.

"She said the boy's father took him into the mountains and she wants to find him."

"Or she misunderstood the rendezvous point. She's probably bringing the stuff back to sell."

"You seriously think she's involved in drug trafficking?"

Gray couldn't believe Katie had become a ruthless drug dealer. *She was a heartbreaker, but not a criminal.*

"It's a possibility," the deputy said. "She could be working with the ex. Rumor has it someone's growing marijuana up by Carter Pass. It's rugged country but perfect for that sort of thing."

"Why haven't the Feds gotten involved?"

"They won't go up there on rumor alone. They'd need proof."

"How can I help?" He couldn't stand the thought of criminals abusing the land.

"Find out what you can from the woman. If you decide to track the boy and ex-husband let me know so I can be ready with backup."

"I can take care of myself." Gray eyed the cabin.

"I don't like that look on your face," Tom said. "Don't play hero."

"Wouldn't think of it. Wish I knew more about the case."

"Here." Tom scribbled something on his pad and

handed it to Gray. "My contact with the Feds. Shoot him an e-mail."

"Thanks."

"Take care, then."

"You, too."

Gray went to the cabin and hesitated on the front porch. This time he was ready for her games. Stepping inside, he hesitated at the sight of her on the sofa, petting Squirt.

"What did the officer want?" she asked.

"Just checking in."

"Does he do that often?"

"Not often. How about a warm-up on the coffee?" He fired up the burner. When she didn't answer he glanced up. She no longer seemed confident or seductive. She nervously fidgeted with her purse. Why? Because the cops were close?

"So, where do you think Anderson took the kid?" he said.

She clutched her bag in her lap. "Tyler. My son's name is Tyler."

Gray waited. He couldn't care, couldn't get involved.

"He talked about taking him to a campground near Bear Lake."

Right on the way to Carter Pass where the deputy said they were growing weed.

"What are you worried about?" Gray said. "Maybe the guy wants some alone time with his son."

He was taunting her, hoping she'd break down and spill the truth.

"Could I get some milk for my coffee?" she asked.

"Sure." He opened the refrigerator and pulled out a half-gallon glass bottle.

When he turned to place it on the counter, he froze. Katie was aiming a .22 pistol at him.

Chapter Two

She looked down the barrel of the pink-lady pistol. Gray's eyes turned from sky-blue to indigo. Dark, angry, threatening. He'd left her no choice.

"What the hell are you doing?" he asked.

"You've got to help me." Her voice shook. She was at the end of her wits, panicked, out of her mind. "He's got my son and I need him back. You don't know what Lee's capable of."

Gray stepped around the counter and started toward her as if she wasn't threatening him with a weapon.

"Don't come any closer," she warned.

"Or what? You'll shoot me?"

"Why won't you help me?" She steadied her trembling fingers on the pistol.

He edged closer, extending his hands in a friendly gesture. "Now, Katie," he said in a patronizing tone, "when you bought that weapon, didn't they tell you never to aim it at someone unless you intended to kill them? Not wound, or maim. Kill. Do you intend to kill me?"

No, not kill. Persuade.

"You have to help me find him," she pleaded.

He lunged, startling her. The gun went off and they hit the floor, Gray pinning her with his body. The pistol sprung from her fingers.

"Off! Get off!"

Pinned, helpless. Never again. She'd promised herself.

She jerked her knee to hit a vulnerable spot, like they'd taught her in self-defense class. Anticipating her move, he rolled off, snatched her gun and went to the kitchen.

"My son is in danger," she pleaded.

"Yeah, from his drug-dealing parents," Gray said over his shoulder.

"I'm not a part of that."

"Uh-huh." His back to her, he slammed the .22 to the kitchen counter and turned on the water.

He'd probably read the guilt in her eyes, guilt that haunted her because she couldn't protect Tyler.

She stared at the ceiling, adrenaline surging through her body. Gray had taken her gun and she needed it to protect herself from her crazy ex-husband.

She climbed into the rocking chair and strategized how to get the gun back. The running water stopped.

"Why are you carrying a firearm?" he said.

"Dad gave it to me to protect myself."

"From?"

"My ex-husband."

"Bull. If your father was that worried, he'd protect you himself."

Gray turned and she gasped at the sight of him holding a bloodied dishrag to his upper left arm.

She stood. "I shot you?"

"That was the idea, wasn't it?"

"No, Adam, I'm sorry, I'm—"

"The name's Gray, not Adam."

"We have to call 9-1-1."

"It's fine."

"You're bleeding." She started toward him.

He put out his hand. "Stay away from me."

"I didn't mean it."

"You aimed a gun and pulled the trigger. You meant it."

"You charged me and it went off by accident. Let me help."

Pulling the rag away from the wound, she saw that the bullet had grazed the skin. "Do you have antibiotic ointment?"

"Now you're Florence Nightingale?"

"Yes or no?" she challenged, staring into his midnight-blue eyes.

"Down there." He nodded toward the bottom cabinet.

She found ointment, gauze and tape.

"You've got a lot of supplies here," she said.

"You never know when an old girlfriend is going to stop by and shoot you."

He couldn't be referring to Katie. Sure, she and Adam had been friends growing up, but she'd never considered him anything more than the shy boy who built forts in the forest.

"This was not supposed to happen," she whispered, trying to apply ointment to his wound through his shirt.

"No? What did you expect was going to happen? You and I would go riding off into the sunset?"

She glanced into his cold, dark eyes. "I'd hoped you'd help me find Tyler. I'd hoped this nightmare would finally be over."

He stared straight ahead as if he couldn't stand the sound of her voice.

"Take off your shirt," she ordered.

"Excuse me?"

"I can't tape this properly."

He stripped off his denim shirt, then his white undershirt. Oh, yes, he *had* changed, she thought, struggling to ignore his firm chest.

She wiped the wound clean, then applied ointment. She bandaged his arm, muscled from years in the military followed by working his land.

She'd give anything to live in an isolated spot like this, away from trouble and surrounded by the peace of nature.

Glancing at Gray, she realized he didn't look a bit peaceful. "I'll go now," she said, applying the last piece of tape.

"You'll wait while I call the deputy and press charges."

She took a step back. "You can't."

He picked up the wall phone.

"Please?" She touched his shoulder. "Tyler is all I've got. If I'm locked up I'll never find him. I just want my boy, and to be free of my ex-husband for good."

He hesitated and hung up the receiver. "Then turn yourself in."

"You think I'm involved in Lee's drug business?"

He clenched his jaw and waited. For what? True confessions?

"Give me my pistol and I'll be on my way," she said.

"If you have nothing to do with your husband's business then you don't need a firearm." He placed the gun in the top drawer with the silverware. "I'll keep this so you don't shoot anyone by accident. Go on, take your lies and your problems and drive away."

Anger burned her insides. This man was her best

chance of finding her son. No, she'd have to find another way.

She went to the door and hesitated, gripping the handle. "I'm truly sorry."

"It's a flesh wound."

"No." She turned and held his gaze. "I'm sorry about whatever happened that made you so...hard and uncaring. Goodbye, Adam."

She shut the cabin door, anxious to get away. Not because she feared he'd call the deputy, but because she couldn't stand being in his company for another minute. She couldn't believe how the military had changed him from a gentle, compassionate boy to a hard, uncaring man.

Don't fool yourself, girl. That transformation started with Hoot's death.

With your betrayal.

Guilt wormed its way into her conscience, guilt for so many things, especially being naive. She'd wanted desperately to believe in solid marriages and happily-ever-afters. When that failed she wanted to end her connection to Lee Anderson so he could never hurt her or Tyler again.

Yet guilt by association had chained her to her ex. Some days she wondered if her own father believed her innocence. She couldn't think about that now. She had to focus on finding Tyler and disappearing so they'd be safe.

God, please don't let her be too late.

GRAY TOSSED AND TURNED for two hours before giving up on sleep.

Ghosts did that to a person. They taunted him, driving him out of bed to the kitchen table, where he threw himself into a wood-carving project. He'd hoped to distract himself from remembering Katie's sweet face, the scent of her hair...

Lilacs. Her hair smelled like the lilac bush outside of the old house on 17th Street.

With his shaping knife he worked on his miniature eagle until early in the morning until his eyes began to blur, making it too dangerous to continue.

He sent an inquiry to the e-mail address Deputy Connor had given him, and dragged his tired ass back to bed. Not that the Feds had to answer his questions. He was a nobody regarding this case, but he wanted background on the chance that...

The chance that what? He let those seductive green eyes talk him into helping her find her kid and reunite with her husband? Not happening.

He couldn't stand being manipulated. What else would you call Katie making the moves on him last night?

Gray couldn't have been asleep more than an hour when someone pounded on his door.

Did he need to post No Trespassing signs around the perimeter of his entire property? More like Do Not Disturb signs, because he'd been disturbed too damned much in the past twelve hours, both by Katie in the flesh, and Katie in his dreams.

Sweet Katie, endearing Katie. Aiming a gun at him.

Bang!

He jerked up in bed, his heart pounding. She'd shot him in the arm last night, then left. Everything was fine. Back to normal.

Bang, bang!

"Enough!" he shouted. He slipped on his jeans, grabbed his rifle from beside the fireplace and marched to the door.

He peeked through the sheers and spied a man, about six-two, his back turned, hovering on the porch. Gray swung open the door.

"Where's my daughter?" The man stormed into Gray's cabin.

"Excuse me?"

"Katie. She was here, wasn't she?"

The man turned, hands on his hips. Gray recognized "Big Bill" Meyers, Katie's dad, a police sergeant from Gray's hometown. Her old man was an imposing SOB who wore plaid flannel shirts that made him look like a lumberjack. Gray also remembered the guy had been a mean drunk.

He looked stoned sober today.

"So help me God, if you hurt her—"

"You've got it backward. She shot me." Gray pointed to his bandage.

"What? I don't believe you."

Gray shut the door and went to the kitchenette. Placing the rifle beside the cabinet, he opened the drawer and pulled out the pink-lady pistol. "Quite a gift you gave your daughter. You should have included some range time."

"You bastard." Meyers charged Gray.

Relying on his aikido training, Gray used the man's momentum to get the advantage. He grabbed Big Bill's hand, twisted and brought him to his knees.

"Let me go," he grunted.

"What, so you can take a shot at me like she did? No thanks."

"Why did she shoot you?"

"Because I said 'no.'"

"Bull," he grunted. "I taught her never to aim at anything she wasn't prepared to destroy."

Gray let go, but held a ready stance. "She wasn't trying to destroy me. She was trying to persuade me to help her."

Her old man stood and shook his hand to get the feeling back. "Where is she now?"

"Took off last night."

"What, without her firearm?"

"I told her I'd hold on to it so she wouldn't accidentally kill someone."

"You son of a bitch, she needs that weapon to defend herself. What's happened to you, boy? Did the army screw you up so much you won't help a girl in distress when she asks for it?"

"I don't owe *that girl* anything."

"Katie—her name is Katie and she's been through hell." He marched to the front window and stared out at the lake. "This is about Hoot, isn't it? You still blame her for his death."

"That was a lifetime ago, Sergeant. Move on. I have."

"Have you?" Meyers turned and pinned Gray with his steely brown eyes. "Katie told me years later that the kids made up the story about Hoot selling them liquor so they wouldn't get into trouble. Katie kept the secret because she wanted to protect her brother from the police." He paused. "And me. God knows what I might have done to him back then if he'd been arrested." He glanced at the floor. "The only reason she was there that night was because she wanted to be liked by the popular kids, especially the football star, Lee Anderson."

"Whom I hear she married."

"Yes. We all thought so highly of Lee, a real charmer. We had no idea he led a secret life." He sighed. "I wish Katie would have confided in me. I've been sober for five years now. I could have helped."

"Maybe she didn't want your help."

"Why, because she was his partner? Don't say that. She'd never get involved in drug dealing."

"But the thought has crossed your mind."

Meyers lifted his chin in defiance. "No."

Gray waited.

"Maybe." He glanced back out the window. "Then my grandson told me how his daddy locked Katie in the closet, how he pushed her against the refrigerator so hard that a glass pitcher cracked open on her head. Whenever I'd ask her about it she'd say 'Lee's got a little temper. I've got it under control.' She'd always been the one in control in our family. A lot of good it did her."

Gray fought back sympathy for Katie. Just because she was abused didn't mean she was innocent.

"Why didn't she come to me for help?" her father whispered.

"Like I said—"

"No. She's not a part of his business. She's a good girl, fell for the wrong guy and now he's got her son. Who knows if we'll ever see him again."

Gray snatched a carton of orange juice from the refrigerator and poured himself a glass. "Call Anderson's parole officer."

"He hasn't missed a meeting yet. Even if he does they're not going to aggressively look for him because it's not a federal case. He could cross the border into Canada before they decided to pursue him."

He studied the man who once terrified him as a kid.

"I know there's history between you and Katie,"

Meyers began. "This has nothing to do with the past. It's about a little boy who's been taken from his mother, your friend Katie."

"I don't have friends."

"What the hell? Do you want me to beg for your help? I will, gladly. I heard what you did in Special Forces, how you survived impossible missions. You've got the skill to find my grandson." He crossed the room.

Gray had faced down plenty of adversaries, but "Big Bill" could still intimidate the hell out of him.

"You can help," Big Bill murmured. "You're a hero."

Gray fisted his hand. "No, sir, I'm no hero."

"That's not how I hear it. I'll pay you whatever you want."

"I don't want your money."

"Then what? What do you want, my family's apologies for putting Hoot in jail? Son, no one could have known he had a weak heart."

"I've got other commitments. Here—" He scribbled Jacob Robinson's name and number on a piece of paper. "Jacob is an excellent tracker. I gave his name to Katie last night."

"There's nothing I can say to change your mind?"

Gray held his gaze. "No, sir."

Keep your distance. Don't get involved, especially not with people you have history with.

"Can you at least tell me which direction Bear Lake is?"

"About four miles north on Route Seven you'll hit a dead end. It's hiking and riding trails from there, about another mile up Bear Mountain to the lake."

"Hiking. Terrific," he muttered. He brushed past Gray and hesitated on the porch. "That little boy is all she's got. My wife left us years ago, my son moved to Chicago and I've always been either an alcoholic or a workaholic. Maybe that's why I didn't see this coming. My grandson is a sweet and intelligent boy. He deserves to be with his mom."

With a nod, Meyers left, got into his car and drove off.

Only then did Gray realize he was fisting his right hand. This wasn't his responsibility. He wasn't a hero—far from it. He did the dirty stuff: neutralized terrorists, saved hostages.

Gray learned how to function without letting emotion cloud his judgment. The one time it had, a hostage nearly got killed.

Yet emotion was eating at him right now. Frustration? Anger? Had to be. A man like Gray didn't feel the other stuff.

He dressed, figuring he'd better start his chores.

My grandson is a sweet and intelligent boy. He deserves to be with his mom.

Meyers's parting shot irritated Gray, like a festering knife wound that didn't want to heal.

Katie had a child, a connection to another living soul, unlike Gray, who made sure he didn't need anyone or anything. He was an automaton who repelled human connections so as not to disappoint or be disappointed.

He'd disappointed Hoot big-time when he didn't stand up for him. Gray had gone along with the group because he'd wanted to be accepted—make that loved—by Katie more than he wanted to help his friend.

What kind of person would do something like that? No hero, that's for sure.

After eight years of service to the U.S. government, Gray still didn't feel he'd earned back a fraction of his personal honor.

It was a good thing Katie left last night, and even better that she'd shot him. The dull pain was a reminder of what she could do to him: make him ignore his better judgment for a pretty face and a sad story.

Gray thought she'd cared about him when they were kids. He'd been a fool. Never again.

Squirt danced around his ankles. "You wanna go out, boy?" He opened the door and Squirt raced out to chase a squirrel.

Gray eyed the surrounding mountain range. Snow was on the way. What kind of idiot would take his kid camping at Bear Lake this time of year? A stupid dope dealer, that's who.

Gray shut the door. Not his problem.

AFTER CHORES, GRAY headed into town for supplies and maybe to ask around and see if Katie had found a guide to lead her up to Bear Lake. He'd given her names of trackers who'd love nothing more than to spend a few days with a pretty woman.

She was still pretty. That hadn't changed in ten years.

He got out of his truck in front of the hardware store and spotted Tom's squad car at the Breakfast Barn next door. Gray went into the store and picked up batteries, nails and lightbulbs. He was checking out when Tom came inside looking for him.

"Deputy," Gray greeted.

"How did it go last night with your female visitor?"

The teenage clerk looked from the deputy to Gray, then back to the deputy. The gossip mill was going to be buzzing today.

"You mean other than her shooting me?" Gray said.

"What?" Tom said.

The clerk dropped the box of nails on the counter. Luckily it was sealed.

"What's the damage?" he asked her.

"Uh, the damage? Oh, yeah, your total is seven-teen fifty-seven."

He pulled out a twenty and placed it on the counter.

"She shot you?" Tom said. "With what?"

"A twenty-two pink lady."

"Where the hell did she get that?"

"Her father gave it to her." Gray took his bag from the clerk and started for the truck. The deputy walked alongside him.

"Her father checked in this morning. Said he's worried about her."

"She can obviously take care of herself if she got a shot off and actually hit me."

"You want to tell me what made her shoot you?"

"I said I wouldn't help her. I have a feeling she's used to getting her way. I kept her gun." Gray smiled.

"I'll issue a warrant for her arrest."

"It was an accident," Gray admitted.

Surprised even himself.

A maroon sedan sped into the parking lot and pulled haphazardly next to them. Katie's father jumped out and marched up to the deputy. "She's gone, and her things, the hotel room, everything's ripped apart."

"Calm down, sir," Tom said.

"I can't calm down. She's out there somewhere,

probably taken by that bastard, and she's defense-less thanks to him." He turned to Gray. "You son of a bitch." And Big Bill Meyers charged.

Chapter Three

Katie's old man slammed Gray against the truck and the sack went flying. Big Bill wanted to kill somebody.

"Hey, knock it off." Tom grabbed the older man's arm.

Meyers wrenched free and threw a punch meant for Gray's jaw, but he turned and it connected with his gunshot wound. The pain sharpened his focus. Gray slugged Meyers in the gut and he crumpled over.

Tom pulled his cuffs from his belt.

"Don't," Gray said.

Meyers stayed down, his shoulders jerking with short, ragged breaths.

Or was he sobbing? Hell. This was Big Bill Meyers, a guy you didn't want to mess with, drunk or sober. Nothing brought him to his knees.

He glanced up, his eyes red. "I should have believed her, I should have helped her."

The man's guilt tore at Gray's conscience.

"Do you want to file assault charges?" Tom asked Gray.

"No."

"You're asking *him* if he wants to file assault charges?" Meyers stood. "It's his fault she's gone. Come look at her hotel room and see what you've done, you bastard."

"Enough," Deputy Connor said. "This isn't Turner's fault."

"I wouldn't have let her leave my place if I'd known she was in real danger," Gray offered.

"Well, now you know," Meyers spat. "Come see for yourself."

"Go on," Gray said to the deputy. "I'll follow in my truck."

Big Bill glared at Gray. "I swear, if he killed her…"

"Back off, Meyers," Tom warned again with a hand to his chest.

Katie. Dead? No, Gray wouldn't accept that.

The deputy and Big Bill got into the squad car and pulled out of the lot. Gray followed, puzzling over this development. Had she betrayed her ex and was being punished?

Why involve the boy? Must be some kind of power struggle between the husband and wife. *Yeah, keep thinking that way, Turner.*

After all, this was Lee Anderson—arrogant, selfish, star of the football team. What did she think she was getting when she married that jerk?

He pulled into the motel lot and saw a group of spectators outside Room 115. Two county police cars pulled into the lot, along with an unmarked Ford. This was more excitement than the town was used to. A kidnapping was big news.

Parting through the crowd, Gray aimed for the room and noticed the door had been kicked in.

"Back up, everyone, or leave the area," a second deputy ordered.

Gray pushed to the front and Tom motioned for him to join them in the room. When he got inside, Tom put his hand on Gray's shoulder. "Don't touch anything."

"Right."

"This is FBI Agent Sam Washburn." Tom introduced a tall, lean man in his midforties.

"Gray Turner," he said, shaking his hand. "You're the agent who answered my e-mail, thanks."

"No problem."

"I'm surprised to see the Feds here so quickly."

"I was involved with her husband's drug arrest."

"Ex-husband," Big Bill corrected. "That bastard," he muttered, glancing around the room.

The place *had* been torn apart. The mattress was shoved haphazardly against the wall, the desk chair splintered into pieces, and clothes were scattered across the floor.

Washburn fingered a light blue bra lying across the television set. Gray wanted to tell him to get his latex-gloved hands off Katie's underwear.

"Check this out," an officer said from the bathroom. Tom went in first, stepped out and nodded for Gray to take a look. The mirror above the sink had been shattered.

Acid churned in Gray's gut.

"Looks like a setup," Agent Washburn muttered.

Big Bill glared at the agent like he was about to break the guy's face.

"What makes you say that?" Gray asked.

"Isn't it obvious? Make it look like a missing persons case to distract us from the true business."

"My daughter is not a drug dealer," Big Bill growled.

Gray got between them and coaxed Washburn away from Big Bill. "Might want to show some respect around the woman's father."

"I'm not here to show respect," Washburn shot back.

"Why are you here, because Deputy Connor said the Feds had no reason to pursue Lee Anderson. Not yet, anyway."

"Anderson may have graduated to more serious crimes. The woman's been under surveillance in the hopes she'll lead us to him. I'd advise you not to interfere, Mr. Turner. These are dangerous people."

The arrogant Fed sauntered across the room to analyze a few of Katie's personal items.

Gray spotted a colorful photograph on the carpet. Squatting, he turned his head to see it better. It was a photo of a smiling Katie wearing mouse ears. He could never forget that sweet smile of hers.

The photograph had been ripped in half. Gray spotted the other half a few inches away of a cute blond kid, also wearing mouse ears. Must be her son. The boy's eyes sparkled with love for his mom.

Together they were enchanting.

He stood. "They couldn't have gone far. How will you proceed?" he asked Tom.

"First I need to determine if the Feds want jurisdiction." He glanced at Washburn.

"I've called in, but no word on whether they're sending a team. This could just be a temper tantrum."

The agent obviously considered Katie a criminal along with her husband.

"We shouldn't waste time," Gray said. "If she's been taken into the mountains I'm your best bet of finding her."

"I can't ask you to do that," Tom said.

"You haven't." He started for the door, blocking out the violent attack on her room.

On Katie. *Damn, don't fall into that trap again.*

"I'll head for the ranger station at Bear Lake. If I make it tonight I'll radio back and let you know what I've found."

"What's it going to cost me?" her father asked.

Gray turned to him. "I'm helping the local authorities. There's no charge."

"I will not take charity."

"Fine, a hundred dollars a day. That's the going rate."

Which was a lie. Gray had done freelance jobs after his military service and been paid six times that amount. But this wasn't a corporate kidnapping. This was little Katie Meyers from Novelty Hill back home, turned ex-Mrs. Lee Anderson.

From the condition of her room something beyond business had happened here. The room screamed of anguish and betrayal.

Gray glanced at Katie's old man. Guilt colored his eyes.

Guilt, yeah, Gray felt some of that. If he'd kept her at his cabin last night instead of threatening her and kicking her out she'd be okay.

She'd be safe.

Then again, Washburn could be right. This could be a scam to convince authorities she was a victim, not a partner in the drug business.

Whatever it was, Gray knew there was more going on than a father taking his son into the mountains.

"The sooner I get started, the better," he said.

And the sooner these people would be out of his life.

FIVE HOURS LATER GRAY was hiking north on a winding trail.

Alone. He'd even left Squirt behind at the Farnsworth place, so he wouldn't be a distraction.

Made no sense to ride a horse up here since he'd have to track on foot. He focused on the trail ahead, keeping an eye out for signs. Signs of civilians; signs of a struggle. The mention of Bear Lake was Gray's only lead.

Her father held firm to his belief that Katie was the victim. Then again, Meyers was a guilty father who'd lost all perspective.

That's what happened when you got too close: you lost your ability to see the truth and protect the people you cared about.

Emotions cloud judgment: leave 'em at the door. It had been his team's motto. He should have had it tattooed on his arm.

The last person Gray had cared about was Hoot. He'd never seen him after that devastating night. It had been dark when they came for Hoot, cuffed him, hauled him to the police station. Gray hadn't said a word in his defense. Damn, why hadn't the old man defended himself?

Being out here, tracking down Katie, was

bringing it all back, especially his mistakes: Gray's betrayal, Hoot's death, Gray's decision to join the military and earn back some small piece of honor, even if it meant getting killed.

He thought dying for his country would ease the guilt of Hoot's death. In some perverted way, Gray was looking for death to relieve his conscience.

But Hoot had taught him too well. Gray relied on his instincts and had survived. Even when he used handguns and assault weapons, he couldn't completely shut out the inquisitive nature of a tracker. Asking questions kept you sharp and focused.

Hoot's wisdom had saved Gray's life more than once during his career with Special Forces.

He glanced at the colorful sky as the sun set over the mountain range. A chill was in the air. In another hour it would be dark and cold. He'd have to make camp, start a fire and continue his search first thing in the morning.

The skin pricked at the base of his neck. He slowed and listened intently. Robins chatted in the distance. Nothing unusual or alarming.

He crouched down, eyeing pika tracks. He followed them with his gaze. Bright red caught his eye in the distance. Slowly approaching, he realized it was a scarf, similar to the red scarf Katie had worn yesterday.

Gray studied the moist earth for clues. He eyed a trail of matted leaves and followed it about thirty feet where it ended abruptly. He scanned the surrounding area. It appeared normal, undisturbed.

A cougar growled in the distance. Something wasn't right. He sensed danger, but not from the cat. Heaviness filled his chest, pressing against his lungs. A familiar feeling he'd relied on many times during combat.

"Katie, where are you?" he whispered.

KATIE STRUGGLED to breathe as her attacker clamped his arm against her throat. Shocked by the ambush in such a majestic setting, she didn't have time to react. And once she clicked into self-defense mode, she found herself staring down the barrel of a gun.

If threatened at gunpoint, act compliant until you find an opening.

"Katie?" Gray called.

She wanted to answer him, but her vocal cords were paralyzed from the pressure against her neck.

"Katie, answer me!"

She panicked. Would her attacker shoot Gray? She couldn't let that happen.

This had to be one of Lee's men, right? She knew they were ruthless, like their leader. Lee had enjoyed taunting her, watching her squirm when he'd talk about teaching his boy to be a strong man like his father. He'd smile and say that as a man Lee would always need Katie, and would have her anytime he felt like it.

Immediately after the assault she should have taken Tyler and fled the state, regardless of custody laws. But then she'd become the criminal hunted by authorities for kidnapping her son.

Her attacker shoved her to the wet earth. "Not a sound," he threatened and disappeared into the woods.

She closed her eyes. How was she going to save her son if she let men like this terrorize her? No, she'd promised herself never to be a victim again.

"Gray, he's got a gun!" she called out, adjusting her bag across her shoulder.

Two shots cracked in the mountain air; one hit the tree beside her and splintered the bark. Her attacker was shooting at her?

She started to shake.

Not a sound, he'd said.

The same words Lee had uttered right before…

With a grunt, she scrambled to the other side of the tree and took two deep breaths.

She sprang to her feet and ran zigzag toward the trail. She would escape, find Tyler and disappear, either with or without help from the Feds.

Eyes burning with determination, she focused on the trail in the distance. She wished she had her gun. Damn Gray.

Suddenly somebody grabbed her and, before she could react, she found herself looking up into

Gray's blue eyes. Fear and rage drained from her body. He put his forefinger to his lips and motioned for her to wedge herself between his body and the sturdy tree trunk.

She gripped his thick wool jacket, breathing in the scent of pine. She felt safe, no longer afraid for her life.

A few minutes passed. He leaned down and whispered, "I'll be right back."

She couldn't let go of his coat.

"Katie, trust me."

She released his jacket and wrapped her arms around her knees. Reality settled across her shoulders: Lee Anderson would never let her go.

What if she couldn't get the evidence that Agent Washburn needed to put Lee away? What if Lee wouldn't release Tyler, or worse, demanded Katie's companionship?

A wave of nausea rose in her chest at the thought of him touching her, kissing her—

She leaned over and got sick. How could she be so naive to have loved such a bastard? No, she hadn't loved him. She'd been in love with the idea of love.

You will always be mine, he'd said on that hot summer night.

The words that had once warmed her now terrorized her. She'd had no control over her life: her father's drinking, her brother's bad choices or her seemingly perfect husband who was, in reality, a monster.

She leaned against the tree trunk and took slow, deep breaths. *Pull yourself together, girl. No time for self-pity.*

She still had her purse slung across her body. Maybe she should call Washburn. And tell him what? She wouldn't call until she had something to report.

"You okay?" Gray asked, standing over her.

"I've been better." She stood and wobbled a little. He gripped her elbow to steady her.

"That man…" she began.

"He took off toward town."

"I'm lucky you showed up when you did."

"Your dad sent me."

"Oh." It wasn't as if Gray would come looking for her on his own.

"What the hell happened here?" he said in a tone that she'd heard so many times from her father.

"I was attacked," she said.

"Where's your guide?"

"I don't have one."

"You came out here alone?"

She ground her teeth. She needed a little compassion right now, not a lecture.

"Jacob Robinson was booked," she explained. "Besides, on the map it looks like a straight shot up the mountain."

I need my son, damn it.

"You never hike in unfamiliar territory alone, especially if you aren't experienced, got it?"

She nodded and studied the wet earth.

"Your dad was out of his mind," he said.

"I told him not to come," she whispered. She didn't want to involve him in this mess.

"Well, he's here, and freaked-out. Your hotel room was ripped apart, like someone was looking for something. You have any idea what?"

"No." She shuddered to think what would have happened if she'd been there when the intruder burst in. She'd left early this morning to meet with a prospective guide. When told he was booked for two days, she decided to take off on her own.

"Let's move." He glanced over his shoulder. "I'm guessing there's some kind of bounty on you…?"

"Probably my ex," she offered.

"You must have something he wants." He hesitated. "Bad."

Other than to destroy her?

"Come on, let's get back to town where you'll be safe."

"No, I have to find Tyler."

"Katie, I promised your father I'd bring you back. Once you're safe I'll track your son."

She eyed him with skepticism.

"Come on." He took her hand and led her back to the trail. He scanned the surrounding woods, his head cocked to the side up as if he heard something.

"What is it?" she asked.

He eyed the sky. "Snow's coming. Sooner than I thought."

"It's not supposed to snow for a few weeks."

"Lots of things aren't supposed to happen." He glanced at her. "But they do."

Like Katie wanting Gray to hold her, protect her from her ex, from the weather, from herself. But a man of Gray's integrity could never care about a weak woman like Katie, a woman who'd break the law if necessary to save her son.

"Better idea. Let's aim for Deception Creek Campgrounds," he said. "They've got a ranger station and communications equipment. We'll contact your dad and tell him you're okay." He eyed her. "And, Katie…?"

"Yes?"

"If there's anything you need to tell me, now would be a good time."

His caring expression seemed genuine. She wanted to tell him about her deal with the Feds, and if that fell through, her plan to run, hide and never be heard from again.

She wished to God she could confide in someone about her other secret.

"Anything," he prompted.

She'd betrayed him before, involved him in a

mess of lies that led to a man's death. She wouldn't do it again. Not to the once-sweet Adam Turner.

"No, there's nothing." She glanced away.

When it was all over, after she'd rescued her son, she'd either be in witness protection, a fugitive or dead. There was no point in involving Gray in that.

"All right, then." Gripping her hand, he led her to the trail. They walked in silence, Katie falling into pace with him. She suspected he walked slower than usual for her sake. So, he still felt compassion? Up to this point he'd shown her nothing but judgment.

She followed close, pretending theirs was a genuine relationship. She couldn't remember the last time she'd felt loved by a man.

Had she ever? Could you call being Lee's showcase wife a loving relationship?

Her son's love, his life, was all that mattered now. What about the other life growing inside of her? A life created of violence and domination?

She would not allow her shame to taint this child's existence. A child was a miracle, a gift.

Picturing Tyler's bright smile gave her strength. She imagined them moving to a nice place like Kansas or Oklahoma, someplace where they could blend in and be anonymous.

It would be lonely, but at least they'd be safe.

"We're not going to make it," he said.

Big, wet snowflakes started to fall. The wind

rushed through the trees, bending the limbs with powerful force.

"We'll have to find a spot to bed down for the night," he said. He eyed the surrounding area, encouraging her to keep up the pace by taking her hand and giving it a squeeze. If anyone could rescue her son it was Gray.

She'd heard stories of his courageous missions. He'd returned to Washington a military hero. Yet he'd seemed offended when she'd referred to him that way, as if he was ashamed about what he had done in the service. Why? He'd defended his country and rescued hostages. She suspected his missions were violent, but that was his job. There was nothing to be ashamed about.

"Over there," he said, motioning to a cabin in distance.

She blinked against the falling snowflakes and heard the unmistakable click of a rifle.

Then another.

Two men stepped onto the trail, the older man aiming a rifle at Gray's chest.

"You can stop right there," the armed man ordered.

Chapter Four

Damn, why hadn't he sensed their presence?

Because Katie was holding his hand, that's why. Clutching it like she needed the connection to breathe.

That connection, even through the gloves, had blown his focus.

He shifted Katie behind him and raised his other hand in surrender. It was his right hand, his firing hand. If he could only get to the Glock, buried beneath his coat.

"My name's Gray Turner. I'm a guide from down below helping this woman look for her little boy."

The leader, a stocky guy pushing fifty, lowered his rifle and motioned for the other guy to do the same. "You should head back."

In one fluid movement, Gray lowered his arm and edged his jacket open. "Why's that?"

"Someone trashed our camp. Everything's

gone—food, equipment. We're heading back to town."

"You're campers?"

"You could call us that." The leader glanced at his buddy and back to Gray. "We heard about gold chip mining up past Deception Pass and thought we'd check it out."

"Did you see the men who ransacked your site?"

"From a distance. We spotted the assault weapons and hightailed it out of there."

"Oh God," Katie whispered, leaning into Gray.

He wished she wouldn't do that, lean into him as if absorbing his strength.

"I'm Hank," the fiftyish man said as he shook Gray's hand. "This is my son, Christopher. Never thought we'd be robbed. Expect that kind of thing in the city." He glanced across the rugged countryside, now blanketed with light snow. "Not out here."

"Robbery is unusual," Gray said. "Did you report it to the park ranger?"

"Haven't seen him since yesterday."

Had Anderson's men taken out the ranger? Rangers didn't have military or police training. They were nature lovers, like Hoot.

"Have you seen any kids out here?" Gray asked.

"Nope," Hank said.

"I saw one," his son offered. "Yesterday, hiking towards Bear Lake with an older guy. I figured it was his father."

Katie's body slumped against him. He squeezed her hand then let go. *It's a game. She's a part of it.*

Hank glanced at the sky. "We'd better head down."

"Might be safer to hang around until the storm passes," Gray offered.

"I'd just as soon head back to town." He blew into his cupped hands.

"Suit yourself." The guy must be really spooked.

"You be careful," Hank offered.

"You, too. There's good shelter by Coogin's Creek. You might consider stopping there."

"Thanks."

"Good luck," Gray said.

The guy nodded, and the two men started down the trail.

Amateurs. He hoped they didn't cause themselves more trouble.

"Do you think we should head back, too?" Katie asked.

He eyed campgrounds dusted with snow. Weather up here could change as quick as a green light to red.

"No, going back will present its own set of problems. Come on, let's find the ranger cabin."

He hoped they could spend the night there; it'd been years since he used his wilderness skills to build shelter. Would he remember how to make something stable that would protect them?

He glanced at Katie. She'd grown pale. Why, because she was stuck spending the night with Gray? *Fool, this has nothing to do with you and everything to do with her finding her son...and husband.*

He'd give anything to know if she was still in love with Anderson. It would help him get his bearings with this objective. Objective? He wasn't with the military anymore. He was a civilian, asked to find a man's daughter and bring her back to safety.

"At least we know your boy's close," he offered, but wasn't sure why. "Let's get to the cabin on the other side of the lake. We can stay there, wait for the storm to pass."

He'd lose precious time taking her down and hiking back up again. Yet he'd made a promise to her dad to bring her back. Being in the mountains surrounded by her ex-husband and his criminal friends was not a safe place for a fragile woman like Katie.

They hiked around the lake to the ranger station. Not only did she look pale, but she seemed distant.

He used to be able to read her so easily when they were kids. As a woman she was a mystery. Definitely hiding something, more than one thing, and she didn't trust him enough to spill it. Of course not. He'd as much as accused her of being a drug dealer last night, then kicked her out.

Katie didn't consider him a friend or confidant. Just a means to an end, like when they were teenagers and he'd shared his secret hideaway with her, perfect for having a party.

Forget the past and focus on your current situation.

Something felt odd about the drug gang robbing Hank's campsite. Did Anderson's soldiers run out of food? Or were they trying to drive away possible witnesses to their activity?

Gray wished he knew if there were other hikers and campers up here, other innocents who could be in danger.

"You're worried they'll come back, aren't you?" she asked.

He looked straight ahead, avoiding her probing eyes. Although he'd lost his ability to read Katie, he suspected she could sense when he was being completely honest. And he couldn't say for sure that Anderson's men wouldn't return.

"I'm not worried." He'd taken out a dozen guys by himself in Costa Rica. He could neutralize a handful of drug dealers.

They reached the cabin, picked the lock and swung open the door to the one-room structure. It had a fireplace and twin bed. It made Gray's cabin look like a five-star hotel.

"Get comfortable, relax," he uttered.

He grabbed a chair and jammed it against the

doorknob. Wooden shutters covered the windows that the ranger probably locked up when he headed down for the winter.

She sat on the bed and slipped a strand of honey-streaked hair behind her ear. She looked tired, beaten.

Gray scanned the room. His gaze settled on the bed. Katie fidgeted as if she thought he was thinking about climbing under the wool blanket....

With her.

That would never happen. She was as manipulative as ever and he wouldn't risk a repeat of their previous disaster: Gray following her like a lapdog, obeying her commands, betraying his friend and betraying himself.

Gray wouldn't be taken like that again.

He shoved back the compassion nagging at him ever since he'd found her running blindly from the bounty hunter. Running, trembling, desperate for Gray to save her.

She knew what kind of business her husband was into. She knew the risks.

He knelt beside the bed, hoping to find the communications gear stored beneath. She clutched that damned bag to her chest as if it were a shield. Her green eyes widened.

"I'm not going to hurt you, Katie," he said. "I'm checking under here for communications equipment." He scanned the floor beneath the bed. Nothing.

Katie glanced around the room. She looked so young, so innocent.

Don't kid yourself, Turner.

"What do you think happened to the ranger?" she said.

"Could have gone down for the season. Or your husband's men could have taken care of him."

He didn't sugarcoat it. He needed the constant reminder that she was connected to a drug dealer. It would help Gray keep his distance.

"Put your feet up, relax," he suggested.

"Relax? With those men out there?"

"Suit yourself."

She hugged her bag tighter to her chest.

"If I'm in the bed, where are you going to sleep?" she squeaked as if she feared he'd say *with you.*

"I don't sleep," he said. "I'll be keeping watch."

"But—"

"Your father's paying me to keep you safe. That's my job."

She glanced away as if hurt that Gray wasn't doing this for himself. Because he cared.

He didn't care. Not about her.

Keep telling yourself that and maybe you'll believe it.

He abhorred criminals and he hated being manipulated. Finding and bringing Katie back would solve both issues, especially if they could lock her up.

For what? Flashing her emerald-green eyes at him and making him want her?

He had to get the hell out of here.

"Secure the door behind me," he ordered.

"Where are you going?"

He ignored her and went around back to get wood for the fire. *Bad idea, Turner.* Smoke drifting up from the chimney could alert predators. But he didn't want Katie to freeze during the night. Damn, his concern for her was messing with his good sense.

Besides, there were other ways to keep warm. Body heat topped the list.

Might as well put a gun to his head. There was no way he'd get involved with Katie, no matter how pretty, or sweet. He'd done enough *complicated* in his life. He wanted simple, easy.

Gray sensed she hid dark secrets, even from her father. Fear and desperation haunted her eyes.

If she wouldn't tell Big Bill, she definitely wouldn't tell Gray. Which complicated matters. It helped to know everything about your mark, including motives, fears and needs, in order to keep the person safe.

All he knew about Katie was that she held something back, something that might put both of them at risk. He also knew she genuinely feared for her son. Why would Anderson take his anger for Katie out on the boy?

Gray went back to the cabin and knocked. "Katie?"

He waited. She cracked the door open and turned her back to him, ambling to a wooden chair by the fireplace.

"You can rest if you want," she said. "I'm too hyped up to sleep. I'll keep watch."

"Uh, thanks, but no, thanks."

"Because you don't trust me?"

"I'm trained in this line of work. You're not."

"I want my gun back," she announced.

He peeked out the window. "Why, so you can shoot me again?"

"Maybe."

When he turned to fire off a wisecrack, he read fear in her eyes. She wasn't afraid of *him,* was she? He'd just saved her from the bounty hunter.

No matter. Her fear would keep her sharp and alert.

"The only one who should have a gun is the person trained to use it," he said.

"I need my gun."

"And I need a cheeseburger. Drop it, Katie. You're not getting your gun back."

"What if I'm attacked again?"

"You won't be. Not while I'm around."

KATIE WANTED TO TAKE solace in his words, but knew they were born of obligation to her father.

Grey sounded irritated. Of course he did. He was the hero, the guy who led teams into rescue missions. He knew his stuff, and she knew nothing. She *was* nothing. She heard the inference in his voice. Then she heard another voice. *Pretty and silent: the perfect wife.*

Lee's words. He'd changed so much over the course of their marriage. How could she have not seen it? Because she lived in fantasyland, content with the high school hero as her husband, the man who always said the right things at dinner parties, to her family, even to her…in the beginning.

And now he'd dragged her son out into this storm somewhere. Tyler would never be safe with his father.

"No one's going to hurt you as long as I'm here," Gray said.

She glanced at his rigid back as he stared outside. Rigid, just like the man.

And honorable. He'd never understand her resolve to do whatever was necessary to save her child, whether it be break the law, run away or—she hated to consider it—kill her husband. She knew Lee's ways, how he mentally abused Tyler, telling him he'd never be man unless he toughened up and stopped being so sensitive. A week ago he'd bought Tyler a pocketknife, ordering him to always keep a weapon handy. Why? Because Lee's competitors would come after his son?

She closed her eyes. "Where would they have gone?"

"Bear Lake is north of here, about four miles," Grey said.

"What's it like?"

"Desolate, rugged. I'd live up there myself but Squirt would never allow it."

Was he joking with her to ease the tension of the last few hours? He had to feel it, too, right? Even a hardened Special Ops guy must have been a little rattled by his tangle with the bounty hunter.

Studying Gray Turner, she realized not much rattled him. This man, this stranger, was nothing like the boy she'd once trusted with her secrets.

She'd been foolish in high school to turn away from Adam, the one person she trusted most, to chase after an illusion.

Gray Turner was no illusion. He was a military hero. A man who couldn't possibly understand how she'd fallen into such a deep hole with her eyes wide open.

Never again. She'd never believe a man's promises. Not that any man would have her now, not in her condition.

She started to tear up. Drat, the hormones were flaring again.

"You okay?"

She glanced at Gray. He'd narrowed his eyes in question, as if trying to read her thoughts.

"I can't go back without him," she said, rubbing her stomach. This child would grow up with a big brother; the baby would grow up feeling safe and loved.

Leaning against the wall, Gray eyed her as if waiting for more. "Him, as in your son? Or your husband?"

Right. Gray still suspected her of being part of Lee's business. She glanced at the cold fireplace. She couldn't stand the way he looked at her with those disappointed blue eyes.

He had no clue what she planned to do.

For his sake she'd keep it that way. Even if she had to endure his censure.

"I'd build a fire but the smoke could draw attention," he said.

"Right."

"Maybe the ranger's got extra blankets around here." Gray searched a wooden cabinet.

"Need help?" she said, trying to be polite.

"No, you need to rest."

She wished he'd stop acting like he cared.

The only thing Gray Turner cared about was taking her back to town and getting his reward from her father. That's probably what he planned to do tomorrow when the weather improved.

"Nothing in here." He turned to her. "I'm going to do some reconnaissance outside. Be right back."

Gray shut the cabin door behind him.

He couldn't stand to be near her. Whatever. She couldn't concern herself with his judgment.

She wasn't going back without Tyler. Tears burned the backs of her eyelids. Time to *toughen up*. She hated the expression, but if she'd been tougher she would have escaped Lee. She would have put her disappearing act into play before Lee got the upper hand.

She'd never give any man the advantage again.

She glanced at Gray's backpack. He had to have an extra gun in there, right? Any kind of gun—at this point it didn't matter. She could shoot well enough to hit an attacker in the chest. Shooting Gray last night had been his fault. If he hadn't lunged at her—

She closed her eyes and took a deep breath. The flashback of her husband's assault darkened her thoughts. He'd lunged. Grabbed. Demanded.

With Tyler in the next room, a little boy who feared his father, she thought it better not to fight Lee and create a violent scene. A violent scene that would make Tyler come running to see what was going on.

Her job was to protect her son.

No matter what.

She went to Gray's backpack and kneeled down.

Peeking inside, she found protein bars, beef jerky and trail mix. She dug to the bottom. No gun.

Opening another section, she glanced over her shoulder. She didn't want to be caught going through his things. Her fingertips touched on cold metal and she pulled something out. Only a flask. She opened and sniffed. Yikes, some kind of whiskey.

She continued to rifle through his things, but didn't find a weapon. Was she going to have to swipe the gun he kept at his waist? Now that would be a trick.

Her eyes caught on a piece of paper, folded and shoved into a side pocket. She slipped it out and her breath caught at the e-mail's subject line: *Anderson connection.*

In my opinion Lee Anderson is into more serious crimes than cannabis production and distribution. I also believe his ex-wife is involved. She's our direct link to Anderson. Through her we can potentially put Anderson out of business and behind bars for life.

Call if you have questions.

Agent Sam Washburn, FBI

She didn't understand. She was working with the Feds in exchange for her and Tyler's new identities. Was this part of Washburn's plan to help her stay undercover? If Agent Washburn thought it necessary to keep Gray in the dark, Katie had better watch herself. She didn't want to spill the truth to someone who could ruin her deal with the Feds.

The e-mail was dated today, which meant Gray was checking up on her, didn't believe that her motivation was simply to get her child back. He probably thought she was trying to rendezvous with her husband.

Fine, everyone knew their roles. She'd play out hers and gain her freedom.

The wind whistled violently outside. An image of Tyler trudging up some remote trail in his sneakers taunted her.

She blamed herself for leaving Tyler alone, but they'd needed milk, and Tyler couldn't be torn away from his video game long enough to go with her on the errand. She'd been gone only minutes. It was as if Lee had been waiting for her to leave so he could snatch Tyler.

Her son was out there in a blizzard, being trained to be tough. Lee wanted to punish Katie; Gray wanted to collect his reward from her father. Everyone had an angle.

She shoved the e-mail into the side pocket of Gray's backpack and went to the door. She swung it open and a gust of wind nearly slammed it shut. Even a hero like Gray couldn't find her son tonight, not in this storm.

Frustration brewed as she waited for him to return. It was time to plan their next move, figure out where Lee had taken Tyler.

Anger tore through her and she raced outside in search of Gray. She couldn't see him through the blinding storm.

"Gray!" she shouted. She struggled to breathe against the fierce wind.

"What are you doing?" He ran up beside her.

"I have to find him, I have to…" Her voice trailed off as her gaze fixed on something in his hand.

Tyler's Seattle Mariners jacket.

"No." Her knees weakened and she swayed.

He gripped her arm. "It's his, isn't it?"

Her vision blurred as she struggled to breathe. She grabbed the jacket, turned and started running toward the trail.

"Katie, stop!"

Have to find him. He'll catch cold without his coat. Why did he take it off?

Because he no longer needed it.

Because…because he's dead.

A strong hand grabbed her arm and swung her around. "Stop, come inside."

"I need to find my boy!" she cried, then felt it again, the nausea she couldn't escape. She raced toward a tree and retched.

A few minutes later she felt his hand on her shoulder. "Are you okay?"

She glanced up at him. "Yes."

"You don't look okay." He placed the back of his hand to her forehead.

She wanted to scream at the gentle touch, a touch she hadn't felt since...since never.

"You're warm. Let's get inside." With an arm around her shoulder, he led her back to the cabin. "We're going back to town as soon as possible. You need medical attention."

"No, I'm fine. I'm just pregnant."

Chapter Five

Gray felt sucker punched to the gut.

Why should that bit of news surprise him?

With an open hand pressed to her back, he guided her toward the cabin. He couldn't spend another hour, much less an entire night, inside the small confines of the cabin with Katie's tearful green eyes looking back at him.

I need my son.

I'm worried what Lee might do.

Lies, all lies.

She was pregnant and hiking through unfamiliar, rugged land to get to Lee Anderson. So consumed with love for that bastard she'd put her unborn child in danger. This was no place for a pregnant woman.

"Gray—"

"Don't," he said, pushing open the cabin door and guiding her inside. He shut the door and grabbed his pack.

"Where are you going?" she said.

"I can't keep watch for Anderson's men from in here. I'll bunk outside."

"In a snowstorm?"

"I've slept in worse."

He couldn't stand the sight of her. He hoped the storm passed quickly so he could drag her butt back down the mountain and into the arms of her trusting father.

"You're leaving because I'm pregnant with Lee's child?"

"My job is to protect you," he said. Cold, emotionless, masking the torment that raged in his chest. "That's what I plan to do." He still hadn't looked at her. He couldn't.

"By abandoning me?"

He spun on her. "I gave my word to protect you and I'll keep it. Just because your integrity is questionable, doesn't mean the rest of us work the same way."

"Bastard."

"Yeah?" He closed the distance between them. "Then you should like me real good since you're pregnant with a bastard's child. Let me ask you something, was it fun making fools of everyone? The FBI, your dad, making them believe you were through with Anderson? What did you do, have a secret rendezvous? Or did he sneak into your house in the middle of the night on the Q.T.?" He touched her golden hair. She jerked back, anger lighting her green eyes. "It was more exciting that way, right? A sexual thrill?"

"A sexual thrill," she repeated.

He curled a strand of golden hair around his forefinger.

"Yeah, it was thrilling how he cornered me in my kitchen," she said through clenched teeth. "He was about as close as you are right now when he ripped off my clothes and took me in broad daylight against my wishes."

He let her hair slip from his finger.

"But I couldn't protest too loudly because Tyler was in the next room and Lee said if he interrupted us he'd be punished." She pinned him with fiery eyes. "Punished for preventing his mother's rape."

Gray took a step back, trying to figure out if this was another one of her games.

"It was thrilling as hell to worry about my son walking in on us, or if the nosey-body Mrs. Langford next door would see us through her kitchen window and report it to the Feds, further solidifying their opinion that I loved my ex-husband and was a part of the drug business. Or was I just his whore?"

Hell, she had to be playing him again.

"That's why I carry the gun." She stared him straight in the eye. "I will kill him if he touches me again." She paused. "But I see in your eyes you don't believe me."

"Believing you hasn't worked out so well for me in the past."

"Fine. Help me find my son. And don't ever make disparaging remarks about my unborn child." She placed an open hand to her stomach. "It's not the baby's fault its father is an SOB and its mother was unable to protect herself."

"Did you report the rape?" He took another step back.

"No."

He shook his head. *Don't fall for this.*

"Who would believe me?" she said. "Hell, you don't believe me."

But a part of him wanted to.

Watch it, Turner. You're being drawn in again.

"You could have left the state," he said.

She went to the bed and sat down. "Ex-cons have parental rights."

"Does your dad know?"

"No." She glanced at him. "I didn't want to disappoint him further."

"Disappoint him?"

"Never mind. I don't want to talk about it. No one knows about the rape or that I'm pregnant. It's better that way."

"Does Anderson know?"

She held his gaze. "No, it would only give him more control over me."

"You're going to run away with your kid, aren't you?"

"It's no concern of yours. Help me find Tyler and our business will be done. You'll never see me again. No one will."

He wasn't one hundred percent sure he believed her story. Something nagged at his brain, something she was holding back, and until she gave it up he had to assume everything she said was a lie.

"Is that it?" he said.

She narrowed her eyes. "You are one cold son of a bitch."

She'd probably been expecting a compassionate reaction like *I'm sorry.* Gray didn't have time for compassion. Not when on assignment.

"I sense you're keeping something from me," he prodded.

"Nothing that concerns you."

"Everything about you concerns me."

"Sure, right." She sighed. "All you need to know is that my husband is violent and he has my son. I could use my pistol back."

"I can't do that."

"Right. Well, I'm tired." She curled up on the twin bed and rolled over, her back to him.

Go to her, you stupid jerk. Rub her back or stroke her hair.

Not good. He wanted to believe her and comfort her, even though he knew she was lying about something, maybe about everything. All to manipulate him. Of course, what better way to earn his sympathy than to claim her husband had raped her?

"Adam," she said.

"Yes?"

"Thanks for saving me today."

"You're welcome."

"Please don't leave me alone."

The wind ripped from his chest. He realized how much he wanted her innocent request to mean more. That's when he knew he was completely losing his perspective where she was concerned.

That could be deadly for them both.

SHE SHOULDN'T HAVE TOLD Gray she was pregnant. The disgust in his eyes ripped open her shame all over again: shame for being unable to defend herself against her domineering ex-husband.

She heard Gray move a chair across the room. He couldn't stand to be near her. Just as well. She was too tempted to fall into the protective arms of a hero right about now.

This hero wouldn't have her, not with Lee's child growing inside her belly.

She focused on her breathing, on imagining a beautiful sunset over the vast ocean. A few years before the divorce she had taken Tyler to the Oregon coast, rented a cottage and made a weekend of it. Lee had promised to follow the next day, but he never showed. She and Tyler had picnicked on the beach, played in the sand and eventually watched the sun go down across the Pacific.

It was breathtaking.

And peaceful.

It calmed her to imagine the brilliance of nature's beauty. Just like the unborn child, safe and beautiful, growing inside of her. The violent act that created it had nothing to do with the baby. Deep down she knew this.

On the outside, where her nerves fluttered at the surface, she let Gray Turner's scornful expression tear at her conscience, reminding her what a failure she'd been.

No more. It was all uphill from here, literally and figuratively. She was determined to be strong, depend on no one but herself and raise her children in a safe and healthy environment.

If she could only get to Tyler.

Gray draped a blanket across her body.

She pretended to be sleeping. Why was he being nice when he obviously loathed the very sight of her?

Gray loathing her was a good thing. He could focus on the job at hand: finding her son. She could keep her head straight and not be distracted by the once gangly boy who'd grown up to be a strong, powerful man.

Lordy, she did not need another one of those in her life.

The door opened with a burst of cold air and shut again.

He left. Figures.

Yet he'd given his word to protect her and bring her back to Dad. She could count on his word.

With that thought she drifted in and out of sleep. Each time she awakened she'd forget where she was for a second and in that second felt calm and balanced.

Then it would all come rushing back.

She drifted off again, dreaming of a Saturday morning at the open-air market, she and Tyler sampling the donuts, the smell of barbecue tantalizing her nostrils.

The door opened with a crash. "Who the hell are you?"

She jerked up and scooted against the wall, pulling her knees to her chest. A tall man with bloodshot eyes and ragged clothing closed in on her.

"Answer me!" he demanded.

She couldn't speak past the fear clogging her throat.

"Step away from her," Gray said from the door.

The guy spun around to face him. Gray pointed a gun at the man's chest.

"Go on." Gray motioned for the intruder to sit by the fireplace.

The stranger did as ordered. Slumping against a wooden chair, he rubbed at his neck.

Gray kicked the door closed with his boot. The guy had been within inches of Katie. The thought of this guy touching her, hurting her, made Gray tighten his grip on his Glock. Damn, he never should have left her alone.

"Who are you and how many are there?" Gray demanded.

"I'm with the park service."

"Sure you are." Gray eyed the guy's disheveled clothing: torn jeans, a light denim jacket and flannel shirt. A wilderness expert would not be caught in the elements wearing such flimsy clothes.

"I'm Mark Grimes, park ranger for this area. A group of guys jumped me and stole my uniform and my wallet. I thought you two might be with them."

He could be one of Anderson's men playing head games with them.

"Where did this happen?" Gray asked.

"North of here, about three miles. I was checking on a couple that had logged into the book on their way up to Bear Lake, but never logged out. It's been two weeks. They'd indicated they were staying only a week. They were the last ones to go up there."

"Where's the log-in book?"

"I brought it in when we got the weather warning. It's in the cabinet over there."

Gray backed up and opened the cabinet door. Katie sat forward on the bed, her fists clenched as if ready for battle.

"You're Gray Turner, the military hero, aren't you?" the guy asked.

Gray eyed him.

"There aren't many people who could navigate their way up here in this kind of weather at this time of night. I'm Jacob Robinson's cousin. He talks about you a lot."

"Does he?" Gray still wasn't convinced.

"He said you're an amazing tracker."

"More of a mercenary than a tracker."

"He said you had the best instincts of anyone he'd ever met. You helped him find the Farnsworth kid when she went missing last spring."

Gray holstered his Glock. Not many people knew of his involvement with that case. He didn't take on local search-and-rescue jobs, but he'd helped with that one as a favor to Jacob. Eight-year-old Jessica Farnsworth had gone missing near Lake Wenatchee and Jacob was a wreck trying to find her. He'd come to Gray for help, and Gray had agreed, as long as they kept his involvement a secret. He didn't like public attention.

Which meant this guy had to be legit.

"Well, you know who I am," Gray said. "This is

Katie Anderson. Her ex-husband took their son up to Bear Lake and she wants to find them."

"Anderson? As in Lee Anderson's wife?" Mark said.

"Ex-wife," she protested.

"He's expecting you."

She glanced at Gray, her eyes cold. "I'll bet he is."

"I heard him talking to the little boy after his men assaulted me and took my stuff. The boy was complaining about missing his mom and Anderson said she was on her way."

Gray shook his head. To think a small part of him believed her innocence in all this.

"Of course he's expecting me. He has my son. He knows I won't stop until I find him."

Silence filled the room.

"How did you get involved in this?" Mark asked Gray.

"Katie disappeared and her father hired me to find her and bring her back to town. I wasn't sure what I'd encounter up here. Now I know."

"A drug gang."

"Yes." He hesitated. "And no. Instinct tells me there's more going on than drug production and distribution."

There, he'd said it. He'd been thinking it for the past twenty-four hours.

"More, like what?" Mark asked.

"Not sure. What do you think?" he directed the question at Katie.

"I have no idea."

"Not even a guess?" he taunted.

"So she *is* a part of the business," Mark confirmed.

"No," she said. "I'm here to find my son."

He wished she'd stop already, stop with the lies and the games. To think she'd make up a lie like being attacked by her husband, knowing what that would do to a guy like Gray...if he believed her. He'd make it his mission to kill Anderson.

"Oh my God," she whispered, eyeing the park ranger. "You're bleeding."

She went to him and examined the back of his neck. It was then Gray noticed the blood.

"Do you have any antiseptic?" she asked Gray.

Her concern bothered him. Because it was an act?

"There's a kit in the cabinet over there," Mark offered.

She went to the wooden cabinet and got a first aid kit.

"Will you be okay to travel when the storm breaks?" Gray asked.

"Sure."

Katie dabbed at his skin, nibbling her lower lip in concentration. What was it about this woman that still fascinated him?

"I want you to take her back to town with you," Gray said.

Katie glared at him.

"What about you?" the ranger said.

"I'm going to track the drug dealers and report their location. If I head down with her I'll lose their trail."

"Makes sense. The danger is up north, not back toward town."

"Not necessarily. A bounty hunter tried to kidnap Katie earlier today. He was headed back down. You'll need to be ready for anything."

"I don't have a firearm."

"I'll loan you one."

Katie packed up the first aid supplies and closed the white plastic box. She started for the door.

"Where are you going?" Gray asked.

"I need to take care of something."

"What?"

"I need to go to the bathroom, if you must know."

"I'll come with you." Gray pushed away from the wall.

"Is that really necessary?"

"Yes."

"You distrust me that much?" she said.

They faced off, inches apart.

"Do what you need to do." She brushed past him, pulled open the door and headed outside.

He glanced at the ranger. "We'll be right back."

Gray stepped outside and noticed that the storm was already subsiding. Good. Tomorrow would be manageable, especially after he unloaded Katie.

A part of him felt guilty about handing her off to the park ranger. After all, he'd given Big Bill his word. But it would make life a helluva lot easier if he didn't have to be distracted by her lies.

And her sweet face.

She stepped inside the outhouse and he waited, giving her distance. Gray eyed the surrounding forest and made his plans. Tomorrow he'd send her down with the ranger, then head into the mountains to find the boy. That poor kid shouldn't suffer because he had idiot parents.

Suddenly the outhouse door opened and Katie raced out.

"Hey!" he called.

She sprinted away from him, holding something to her ear. Gray ran after her. He was close enough to hear her shout into the phone, "Lee? Lee, are you there? I'm at the Deception Creek ranger station. Lee!"

He grabbed her arm and spun her around.

"Let go of me!" she demanded.

"Telling your lover where you are? Nice."

"I want him to bring Tyler."

"Right. Stop with the lies." He led her back to the cabin. "Just stop talking, period."

They went inside and he slammed the door. "Give me the cell phone."

"What's going on?" Mark said.

"I caught her talking to her husband, although God only knows how she got reception."

"It's spotty up here," Mark said. "But it happens."

"She gave him our location. We need to move. Now."

"In a snowstorm?" Mark asked.

"It's easing up. Besides, she's given us no choice. The sooner we get her back to town the safer we'll be.

"Phone." He put out his hand.

She plopped it in his palm and crossed her arms over her chest.

"Let's pack it up. You strong enough to travel?" he asked Mark.

"I think so."

He couldn't bring himself to ask Katie. She shouldn't be out here in her condition in the first place.

He shouldn't care.

"Let's move." Gray opened the door.

The back of his neck bristled and that heaviness filled his chest. Gray hit the floor just as a gunshot sailed above his head and a bullet splintered the wood door.

Chapter Six

Gray kicked the door shut. His instinct had been razor sharp to sense the threat of a gunman.

"You've been shot." Katie kneeled beside him.

"No, it was a warning to let us know they're out there." He narrowed his eyes at her. "Your man didn't waste any time coming to your rescue."

"I didn't call him, Gray. My phone rang and I recognized the caller ID, but I couldn't hear him. I didn't talk to him."

"Save it."

He sat up and rubbed the back of his head where it had connected with the wood floor. "We're easy targets. We leave this cabin, we're like a bright red bull's-eye."

"What do they want?" Mark asked.

"Her." Gray nodded at Katie. "We'll wait it out. They'll lose patience and come in after us."

"You want them to do that?" Mark said.

"Yes, it will give me the chance to know what we're up against. I'll play injured on the floor. You two stay in the corner."

"What are you going to do?" Katie asked.

What, was she afraid he'd hurt her precious ex-husband?

"I'll do what's necessary."

Mark led Katie to the far corner of the cabin and waited. Gray calmed his breathing, fisted his hands, readied for the attack.

He'd done this many times before, held his position, strategized and waited for the ideal moment to strike. This strategy would have to be timed perfectly.

Or he'd end up with a bullet to his head.

He took a deep breath, focused on bringing his body to complete consciousness. Then he heard Katie squeak and his concentration was blown to hell. The question from earlier started eating at him again: Who would have hired a bounty hunter to find her? If she'd been planning to rendezvous with Lee, he wouldn't send one of his men to bring her in.

Stop. Refocus on the shooter or shooters outside.

"Gray," she whispered.

"Shh."

A few minutes passed, adrenaline rushing through Gray's bloodstream.

"Can't hide all night," a man called from the other side of the door. "Come on out."

Katie and Mark kept quiet.

"I'm here for the woman."

Over my dead body.

Where did that come from?

Because somewhere, buried beneath the lies and manipulations, was the sweet Katie from down the street, the girl he'd lost his heart to over ten years ago. He'd protect her and see her safely into her father's arms, in honor of that memory.

Then he was done.

"I'm coming in."

The door swung open and the knob hit the wall with a thud. Gray felt the man's presence as he hesitated over Gray's still body.

"Oops. Didn't mean to shoot him." The man leaned closer. *Wait for it…*

In a fluid movement, Gray knocked the gun from the attacker's hand and yanked his wrist, bringing him down. Gray flipped him onto his back, slipped his knife from his boot and pressed it to the bounty hunter's neck.

"You again," Gray said. "How many are out there?"

"There's no one else."

"Try again." Gray twisted the guy's hand and he yelped.

"Just me, I swear."

"Who hired you?"

"Screw you."

"No, thanks." Gray twisted the guy's wrist again and he cried out.

Katie turned away. Why? It wasn't as if she hadn't seen her share of violence.

"A name," Gray demanded.

"Fox. Wade Fox."

"Who the hell is that?"

"Drug dealer."

"Does he work for Anderson?"

"Competitor," he groaned.

"Why is he after the woman?"

"Fox wants to hold her hostage to stop Anderson from crossing the border."

"They're fleeing to Canada?"

Clenching his teeth against the pain, the guy nodded.

"Get up." Gray pulled him to his feet and shoved him to a wooden chair. "In my pack is nylon cord," he said to the ranger.

While Mark dug into the backpack, Gray glanced at Katie. She hugged her midsection, her skin pale, her expression defeated.

Sure she was defeated: her lover was abandoning her, escaping into Canada with their son.

Mark handed Gray the cord.

"You're the one who tossed her room?" Gray ventured, binding the intruder.

"Yeah."

"Why?"

"Had to figure out where she was going."

Gray tightened the cord around his wrists in a knot that could hold him for days. He took a step back.

"Why does your boss want to stop Anderson from crossing the line?" Gray said.

"Anderson's working on a hybrid hallucinogenic and Fox wants in on it."

Gray searched the guy and found a high-frequency radio. "We could use this."

Gray paced to the door. "Watch him," he ordered, and stepped onto the porch for better reception. He kept the bounty hunter in his sight. He wouldn't risk leaving Katie alone with him again.

He called the emergency number.

"Nine-one-one emergency."

"This is Gray Turner. Tell Deputy Connor I've found Katie Anderson. I'm sending her and Park Ranger Mark Grimes down and need a team to meet them on the trail."

"Which trail, sir?"

"The hiking trail to Deception Creek Campgrounds."

"One moment, sir."

Gray took a deep breath. He had to stop Anderson and his men from leaving the country. They'd be harder to track once they crossed the line.

Admit it, you want to nail the bastard because Katie still loves him.

"Gray? It's Tom. What's the situation?"

"I've got Katie Meyers up here at Deception Creek. The park ranger was assaulted, but he's okay. We were attacked by a bounty hunter. There might be more out here."

"A bounty hunter?" a different voice said.

"Who's this?"

"Agent Washburn."

"Apparently a competing drug dealer has put out a bounty on Katie Anderson. Wants to use her as leverage to keep Lee Anderson from crossing into Canada."

"I knew she was in this with her husband," the Fed confirmed.

Gray didn't follow that reasoning.

"Hang tight, Gray," Tom said. "We'll send up a team tomorrow morning."

"Can't wait. I suspect Anderson's gang isn't far off. Between Anderson's men and the competing drug gang, there's too much danger up here. I need some men to meet us halfway down the trail. Can you do that?"

He heard low muttering on the other end of the line. "Yeah, we'll send up a search-and-rescue team."

"Someone needs to be armed."

"I'll be with them," Washburn said.

"I'll bring them partway down, then I'm heading back up to track Anderson."

"By yourself?" Tom said.

"They won't sense my presence. I'll locate their position and call it in. Luckily our bounty hunter carries a high-powered radio with him."

"You think they're close to the border?" Washburn said.

"I think they're still in the area, but they're headed for Canada. We ran into campers earlier who saw them this afternoon by Bear Lake. I'm sure Anderson and his men aren't skilled enough to travel at night. They'll stay put until morning, which will give me time to find them."

He wished he could start up now, but he wouldn't risk sending Katie down with a wounded park ranger and bounty hunter.

"Lock the bounty hunter in the cabin and send the woman down with the ranger," Agent Washburn said.

"No can do, sir. I gave my word to keep Katie safe."

More discussion filtered through the radio. Damn, every minute put him that much farther behind Anderson's gang. Gray figured it would take about five hours of night hiking to track them.

"We're sending a team up now," Washburn said. "They'll meet you halfway so you don't lose too much time."

Grey switched off the radio and went into the cabin. Katie stood in the corner, while Grimes hovered over the bounty hunter.

"It's all set," Gray said. "We're heading down. A team's going to meet us."

They packed up and left the cabin. He paired Katie with Mark, the ranger. Gray kept a firm grip on the cord attached to the bounty hunter's wrists.

"You two go on ahead," Gray ordered Katie and Mark. "We'll follow."

THEY HIKED IN SILENCE for about an hour. The storm front had passed quickly, moving east of the mountains. It didn't surprise Gray since weather up here was as predictable as a roulette table in Las Vegas.

His prisoner stumbled and Gray pulled him to his feet. "Don't be stupid," he threatened.

Gray stayed on red alert thanks to the bounty hunter's presence. Suddenly Gray spotted an odd track.

"Hold up," he ordered. He tied the bounty hunter to a tree and knelt to analyze the track: a boy's footprint. Her son's?

"What is it?" Katie asked.

"Not sure. Let's keep moving." He untied their prisoner and started walking.

Puzzling. If the footprint was fresh, that meant the boy might have escaped his father. Gray's priorities shifted. A ten-year-old was more important than nailing Anderson.

Gray wasn't telling Katie about this clue. He needed to keep her in the dark in order to manage this mission.

Hell, Turner, you're not in the military anymore. This was supposed to be a simple search-and-rescue job and he'd ended up working for the Feds.

No, Gray Turner worked for himself. His goal was the boy's safety, which didn't mean he and Katie were necessarily on the same side.

They hiked single file, which kept Katie out of his sight and off his mind.

Who are you kidding?

With every step, every switchback they turned, Gray's senses grew more acute, as if the cool mountain air was awakening something buried for a decade.

Every action affects every living being around it, Hoot used to say. Gray had buried Hoot's pearls of wisdom deep in the recesses of his soul. Yet some of them hovered close in order for Gray to stay alive during his years with Special Forces. He'd survived the infamous death missions that typically caused more casualties than boasted survivors.

Gray found himself needing Hoot's sage advice as he led the ranger, Katie and the bounty hunter down the trail and away from danger.

He hoped that's where he was leading them.

Or had Anderson's competitor planted more thugs in town awaiting Katie's return?

"How are you doing, Katie?" he asked. He wasn't a coldhearted bastard after all.

"Fine, fine."

But she wasn't fine. Katie was moving in the wrong direction, away from her son. She was cold, tired and frustrated.

She knew Gray could find Tyler faster without baggage.

That's what he considered her. She read it in his eyes. She was his baggage on this mission, and baggage from his past.

"Hold up," he ordered.

She stopped and he came up behind her, his scent teasing her.

"You two, get up behind that boulder," he ordered, then turned to the bounty hunter. "You keep your mouth shut."

Gray tied him to a tree while the ranger and Katie took cover.

"Watch her," Gray ordered.

So, he *did* care? Or was he afraid she'd try and make a break for it?

Gray vanished into the woods. How did he do that, seemingly disappear into the mist?

She blew into her hands to warm them, wishing she was safe with Tyler, sitting beside a fireplace somewhere.

The image of Gray's cabin popped into her thoughts. Not an option and she knew it.

He hated her. He judged her.

She was tired of being judged, yet she hadn't let go of her self-judgment for the bad choices she'd made. She wanted her self-condemnation to stop, and the only way she'd do that was to get her son back.

"Stop right there," Gray said.

She heard his voice, but couldn't see him from her spot behind the boulder.

"Turner?" Agent Washburn said.

"How the hell did you get up here so quickly?" Grey asked.

She peeked around the corner and spotted him step back onto the trail.

"They had a secret weapon," a voice said.

"I should have known," Gray said. "It's good to see you, Jacob."

She assumed it was Jacob Robinson, the guide who'd been unable to help her that morning.

Mark climbed out from behind the boulder. "Hey, Cuz."

"What the hell happened to you?" Jacob said.

Katie stepped out from her hidden spot and watched them embrace.

"I'm fine," Mark said.

"All this fuss caused by that cute little blonde that came looking for me this morning?" Jacob asked.

"'Fraid so," Gray said. "She headed up here on her own."

Katie edged her way down from the boulder. She noticed Washburn was with them, along with two other men she didn't recognize.

"I told you I was available day after tomorrow," Jacob said.

"I couldn't wait," she said.

"Used to getting her way," Gray added.

Jerk.

"The bounty hunter is over there, tied to a tree," Gray said. "Where's Deputy Connor?"

"He's managing the case from down below," Washburn said. "We'll take the bounty hunter and the girl off your hands."

Gray hesitated and Katie wondered why. Then he turned to her and extended his gloved hand. "Come on down from there."

She took a few steps and stumbled into his chest. "Sorry." She pushed away from him, secretly wishing she could linger a second longer, inhale the man's scent, his strength. It would undoubtedly be the last time she'd see him.

"What the hell happened up there?" Jacob asked.

"I'll let your cousin fill you in," Gray said. "I can't afford to waste any more time."

Sure, of course he would consider time spent with Katie a waste.

She brushed past him and stepped up beside Agent Washburn.

"Well, at least we've got one of you," Washburn said.

She fought back the shame coursing through her at his tone. But this was part of the act. If the Feds treated her like a criminal, then no one would suspect she was working with them to nail her ex.

Gray took a step closer and she thought he might defend her honor.

"Be careful with this one," he said, eyeing her.

Her heart sank.

"Are we going?" she said, turning toward the trail. She had to get away from him, away from his accusatory tone.

"Hang on," Washburn ordered.

She froze, but didn't turn around. She couldn't stand to look at Gray Turner one more time. He'd bring her son back safely and for that she'd be grateful.

"Turner, this is Agent Ralph Tindle. He's assigned to my team and he's got wilderness search-and-rescue experience. I want you to take him with you."

"No."

She turned at the firm tone of his voice. Gray was studying her, not looking at Washburn.

"What do you mean, no?" Washburn questioned.

"No offense, Agent Tindle, but you'll slow me down."

"This is an official investigation," Washburn said.

"We need a federal officer present when you locate Anderson to ensure proper procedure."

Gray ripped his gaze from Katie and glared at Washburn. "Meaning what?"

"I made some calls. I know what you did in Special Forces. I need my perps alive. Tindle will make sure of it."

Gray glanced at Katie and for a second she thought she read regret in his eyes. Regret at being a trained killer. She didn't see it that way. Gray knew how to protect the innocents and destroy the threats. That was his job.

"I'm no longer in the military," he said. "I don't take orders. From anyone."

"It can't hurt to have someone watching your back, can it?" Washburn said.

"I don't need anyone watching my back, thanks."

"You have no choice."

"No?" Gray eyed Washburn, then glanced at Tindle. "Do what you have to do. I'm not waiting for him. If he falls behind, he's on his own."

"He won't."

Tindle still hadn't spoken.

"What's your motivation in all this, anyway?" Washburn asked Gray. "Money?"

"I'm not taking money for this assignment. I'm in it for the boy."

His eyes penetrated deep into Katie's. He did care.

"I detest child abuse," he added. "Anyone who uses the boy as leverage falls into that category."

He'd find Tyler and bring him back. Katie wouldn't have to confront her husband. Relief settled across her shoulders.

"I'm gone." He nodded at Katie, and started up the trail.

Something broke inside of her. Maybe that last piece of her childhood had finally fallen away.

She started down the trail with the others, pensive, giving a silent thanks that Gray had taken it upon himself to find Tyler.

Then she said a silent prayer for Gray's safety. She didn't want to see him hurt, even if he'd gone out of his way to hurt her.

TWO HOURS LATER Katie was at the police station, a blanket wrapped around her shoulders. Dad had been waiting, and he gave her a big hug and asked if she'd eaten in the past twelve hours. She hadn't eaten much so he'd gone in search of hot food.

For once she was grateful that he was there.

Deputy Connor asked her a few questions and she answered, but her mind was on her son, the dark, cold wilderness and Gray.

He'd get to Tyler. She knew he would.

"Mrs. Anderson?"

She glanced up at the deputy. He'd asked her a

question. "I'm sorry. I'm exhausted. Could I use your bathroom?"

She was actually looking for an excuse to get Washburn alone to see if she could still bargain her freedom out of the Feds. She doubted it. She hadn't brought him any solid information about Lee's location. But still, she had to try.

"The bathroom's down the hall to the left." Deputy Connor smiled. A nice, gentle man.

She thanked him and went in search of Washburn. She knew the Feds had set up their command center somewhere in the building. She shuddered as she approached the cells, the bars solid and intimidating.

A man's voice echoed down the hall. "What do you mean you've lost him?"

"He's former Special Ops, sir," a voice said over the radio.

"I don't care. Find him and you'll find Anderson. Call me with his whereabouts and I'll send in a team to invade the camp."

"What about the boy?"

"Your priority is Anderson."

Air rushed from her lungs. He made it sound as though Tyler's safety was incidental.

"And Turner?" the voice asked.

"If he gets in your way, neutralize him," Washburn ordered.

She wavered, leaning into the wall. So Tyler was

not a priority, and the only person who could help him would be neutralized? Meaning what? Kill him?

Sure, why not, no one would miss Gray, the reclusive military hero. He had no family, few friends and he was in this dangerous situation because of her, her love for her child.

"What are you doing here?" Washburn demanded from down the hallway.

Chapter Seven

Katie doubled over, clutching her stomach. She couldn't let Washburn know she'd heard him.

"I was looking for…for the bathroom…but I think I need to get to the hospital."

Washburn glared at her. He wasn't buying it.

"Help! Somebody help me!" she cried.

"What's going on?" Deputy Connor asked, rushing into the hall.

Washburn begrudgingly went to her, acting as if he cared.

"My baby, something's wrong," she said.

"A baby?" Connor went to her and cupped her elbow.

Good, she could use the shock value to her advantage. He would believe her. He had no reason not to.

"A few months pregnant," she muttered through labored breathing.

"I'll get you to the twenty-four-hour clinic," the deputy offered.

Ignoring Washburn completely, she shuffled down the hall beside the deputy. Now what? Washburn wasn't stupid. He'd figured out that she'd overheard his order to neutralize Gray.

Guilt coursed through her. She shouldn't have involved her childhood friend in this. Now his life was in danger and he didn't even know it.

She needed an ally and quick. She needed to get word to Gray that he was expendable.

Deputy Connor led her into the waiting area. She wished she could confide in this gentle man, but why would he believe her? Who knew what lies Washburn had spun about her criminal history?

She glanced outside and spotted Jacob Robinson and his cousin having a conversation by a pickup truck.

"I'll call emergency," Deputy Connor said.

"No, I don't have good health insurance," she lied. "Can't Jacob take me to the clinic?"

"Okay, sure. Take a seat." He guided her to a chair and went outside. She hugged her belly and pretended to be in pain while determination surged through her. She had to be strong. She would get it right for once, act in time to save her son and her friend.

"Anderson's baby, huh?"

Her gaze snapped up at the sound of Washburn's

voice. He stood in the doorway, looking down on her. "Figures. You've been playing me all along, haven't you?"

The station door opened. "You need help, Mrs. Anderson?" Jacob said.

She sighed with relief. She didn't want to get into it with Washburn. "Just a ride, actually, to your clinic," she said to Jacob.

"No problem." He extended his hand and she grasped it, keeping the other hand against her tummy.

"Wait a second." Washburn blocked her. "I'll stop by later to check on you, and bring you back where you belong."

Jacob and the deputy looked questioningly at Washburn.

"If she's released from the clinic, we'll hold her in a cell until we get this sorted out. After all, she'll be safe in a cell." He glanced at Jacob. "Stay with her until I can relieve you."

Jacob put his arm around Katie. "Come on. Let's get you to a doctor."

"Tell my dad what happened?" she asked the deputy.

"Of course."

Jacob and Mark escorted her to the pickup truck.

"Good luck, ma'am," Mark said.

"Thanks."

He shut the door and they pulled away from the curb, slowly.

"Jacob," she said, "I need your help."

"What's wrong?" He eyed her belly.

"Nothing, the baby's fine. I lied back there."

"Excuse me?"

"I overheard Washburn order his agent to neutralize Gray if he got in the way, and invade my ex-husband's camp. My son is there and could be hurt."

"What? That can't be right."

"I know what I heard."

"Sorry to question you, miss, but…uh…"

"What, you think I'm a criminal, too?"

"No, that's not it, but you've been through a lot today and—" He glanced at her stomach.

"I'm pregnant, not psychotic." She sighed in frustration. "Look, I need to get word to Gray. How can I do that?"

"I think the Fed gave him a communications device, but I don't know the number. Wait, he always wears an emergency locator in case he's injured. There's a chance we could connect with that frequency, setting off the alarm."

"Can you do that?"

"It's possible."

"But he won't know what we're alerting him to."

"He's a smart guy. Just the fact that it's going off will alert him to danger."

"Can you think of any other way to get to Bear Lake? By car, by helicopter, anything?"

He looked at her like she'd gone completely insane.

"This is my son we're talking about." And Gray. A hero who didn't deserve to die this way.

"No," he said.

She slumped against the seat. What was she thinking? If there were another way to get up there Gray would have surely known about it.

"Maybe," he offered.

She sat up. "What do you mean?"

"I shouldn't be telling you this."

"Like, who am I going to tell? The Feds want to put me away, remember?"

"About that, are you—"

"I'm not part of Lee's business, but everyone thinks I am because I didn't turn him in."

"Oh."

"Look, do you know a quick way to get to Bear Lake or not?"

"I discovered some caves that lead through the northern entrance to Bear Lake when I was on the Farnsworth case a few months back. I spotted gold chips so I didn't go public. I've got my reasons." He glanced at her. "Pathetic, huh?"

Who was she to judge? "No more pathetic than me being pregnant with my ex-husband's child."

"Can I ask you something?" he said.

"Sure."

"I understand your worry about your son and all, but why do you care so much about Gray?"

"We have a history. I owe him."

"Yeah, I kind of owe him, too. He helped me find Jessica Farnsworth." He paused. "She's, uh, special to me."

Katie didn't press. They all were entitled to their secrets.

"Let's go to my place and pack some gear. I'll get us as close as possible to the caves, then we'll send a warning."

"Can't we go after him?"

"Only as a last resort. I don't know exactly where the cave lets out in relationship to your husband's camp. It might be dangerous."

Katie would take that chance. Playing it safe was not going to get her closer to saving Tyler, or helping Gray. She was a strong, healthy woman. Heck, she'd taken an aerobics class clear into her seventh month when she was pregnant with Tyler. She wasn't worried about losing this child. She was strong; the doctor had said her pregnancy was un-remarkable.

She wouldn't let Jacob know of her plans to track down Gray herself, if it came to that. He might freak out, take her back.

But she couldn't be in jail, not with Tyler at his

father's mercy and Gray in danger. This was her mess. She was determined to clean it up.

GRAY FIGURED HE WAS maybe half a mile from Bear Lake. If Anderson and his thugs camped there this mission was nearly over.

This mission. Which was what, exactly? Besides purge Katie Meyers from his mind? He'd been so easily drawn in again by her vulnerability and sad smile.

I'm just pregnant.

Just?

She'd fooled everyone into thinking she was through with her ex. Gray was glad she was out of his life.

Almost out of his life. He still had to find her child and help put away her husband.

Ex-husband she'd correct if she were here. But she wasn't here and neither, it seemed, was Gray's shadow, Agent Tindle. The agent had followed him for the past few hours. Probably wasn't a bad idea to have him there in an official capacity.

It would prevent Gray from doing something stupid like taking out his rage on Lee Anderson for involving an innocent kid in this mess.

He and Katie deserved each other.

Agent Tindle had been following a bit too close if his plan had been to remain invisible. Gray knew where he was until twenty minutes ago.

Did the guy misstep and fall over the edge? Or had he been attacked by one of Anderson's men?

This was why Gray liked to work alone, not having to worry about anyone else's safety. He honestly didn't care what happened to Anderson. Gray would snatch the boy, get him to safety and notify the Feds. He figured his shadow had a communications device and would call in their location.

Gray hesitated and turned to look behind him. Where had the agent gone?

Don't assume you understand your surroundings. Always be watchful; be curious.

It was Hoot's voice, a memory from childhood. He rarely thought about Hoot, and then Katie showed up on his doorstep and it all rushed back: the lessons, the wisdom, the betrayal.

Be watchful; be curious.

The hair bristled on the back of his neck and he started to turn when something whacked him across the head. He fell to his knees and sensed another blow coming.

Gray lunged forward, not seeing his target but sensing it just the same. He connected with a man's legs and brought him down on his back. Gray scrambled to pin the guy, but his assailant pushed him off with a knee to his gut. Gray tumbled away, then got to his feet. In a crouched stance, Gray readied for battle.

Agent Tindle aimed a gun at him.

"What the hell?" Gray accused.

Without a word of explanation Tindle fired, hitting Gray in the shoulder. He stumbled back. Something penetrated his jacket and imbedded itself into his shoulder.

Furious that he'd been bested by this jerk, Gray charged him before he could get off another shot. They rolled to the edge of the trail, a steep drop threatening from below.

"What's this about?" Gray demanded, an arm pressed against Tindle's neck.

"Orders," the man choked out, then nailed Gray in the ribs with the heel of his palm, hitting a pressure point that only a trained martial arts expert would know.

Gray should have seen it coming, but the altitude was getting to him, blurring his usually sharp senses.

Or was it something else?

Gray recoiled from the blow and lay motionless. He'd play wounded in order to get the advantage.

"You should have given up, soldier, and I wouldn't have to do this."

Out of the corner of his eye, Gray spied Tindle reaching for him. Gray scissored his legs around Tindle's ankles and twisted. Tindle lost his balance, reaching out for a tree branch and missing. Gray released the hold and followed up with a sharp kick to his shin.

"Son of a—" Tindle stumbled backward and disappeared into the black abyss.

With ragged breaths, Gray crawled to the edge of the trail and looked down. Nothing.

"Tindle?"

His voice echoed back at him.

Gray collapsed and struggled to focus. Had he hit his head when Tindle took him down? His mind was suspended in a foggy blur. Then he remembered the shot Tindle got off before he took a header down the mountain.

Gray unbuttoned his jacket and the top few buttons of his flannel shirt. He slipped his hand against his skin and pulled a short, thick needle from his shoulder. What the hell was this? The guy nailed him with…with what? His vision blurred and the needle slipped from his fingers.

Breathe, Adam. Listen to the whispers of the mountains.

Gray couldn't hear anything but his own panic. He lay no more than half a mile from where Anderson and his drug gang camped. It had started to snow again, softly at first, but had picked up as they'd climbed higher.

No one would find him here except for the druggies on recon. They'd find Gray passed out and vulnerable.

"Have to get…" he muttered. It became harder to form words.

On hands and knees he started toward a spot he'd seen on his way up here—not far, a large tree had fallen and cut across a small, flat section of the mountain. It would have made a good place to camp if he weren't in a hurry to find Lee Anderson, to find Katie's son.

Katie. Sweet Katie, turned criminal.

"Shelter," he said, to keep himself awake. He crawled down the trail, rocks digging into his bare hands. He'd taken off his gloves to remove the needle. Needle? What was it? Had he been poisoned? Didn't see it coming. Failure as a tracker.

Failure as a friend.

He spotted the downed tree in the distance but it kept moving farther away. He'd crawl closer, the tree would float away, out of reach.

Relax, breathe in the pine. Embrace your surroundings.

"Hoot," he whispered. "I'm sorry."

Closer. Farther. The tree kept moving.

One hand in front of the other, he crawled forward, no, backward, no...

He leaned on his left hand and it gave way. He went down, rolling onto his back.

"So beautiful," he whispered as the snow fell, light flakes melting against his skin.

No longer cold...couldn't feel his body.

Floating, drifting. Damn, he'd been drugged.

Couldn't do anything about it. No one could help.

There is always help. All around you, Hoot whispered.

Gray hadn't helped Hoot. He hadn't defended him or exposed Katie and her friends for lying. Couldn't get Katie in trouble. She wouldn't like him anymore.

She'd never talk to him again. He'd never hear that infectious laugh or be warmed by that gentle smile.

He could see her, right here in front of him, emerald eyes sparkling like jewels.

She reached out…she was going to warm his cheek with her hand…

Then the glint of a knife caught his eye. She swung down…

Nailing Hoot in the chest. Killing him.

Hoot. Dead. Katie killed him.

Then it was Gray standing there with the bloody knife. Hoot's blood. Gray felt it all around him, stretched out his hand, covered in warm, sticky blood.

"Get it off! Off!" But it soaked his clothes, burning through to his skin. His mentor's blood burned like acid eating at Gray's flesh.

He frantically ripped off his pack, his jacket and his shirt, but the blood seeped through his shirt and his jeans. All red, wet and burning his skin.

"Get off!" He leaned against the mountain wall and shucked his jeans, then ripped off his undershirt.

It was no use. His legs were stained deep crimson. Blood caked his skin all the way up his chest, like a hardened shell.

Breathe, he had to breathe, but the acid seeped through to the inside of his chest, eating away at his lungs.

"Hoot." He fell to his knees and slugged at his chest, trying to break the shell encasing his skin.

"Hoot," he muttered, digging his hands into wet dirt to try and ground himself.

He wanted it over. Wanted to die.

It is not your time, Hoot said.

Chapter Eight

"How close?" Katie asked. They'd been driving up an uneven trail for at least an hour.

"About half a mile away. No one comes up here anymore. It's been closed by the forest service," Jacob said.

Panic settled low. Something was terribly wrong. She could feel it.

"You okay?" he asked.

"No. Gray and my son are in danger and all I can do is send him a beeper signal he could very well dismiss as malfunctioning equipment."

"He's a smart guy." He glanced into his rearview, then back to the road. "Damn, where did he come from?"

She glanced over the seat and spotted headlights. "Who is it?"

"I don't know, but it can't be good."

"Great, it's probably the Feds." She squared off

at him. "They'll take me back and I won't be able to help Tyler or Gray."

"What do they have on you, anyway?"

Washburn would probably lock her up to perpetuate her role as partner in her husband's business. Or was he going to lock her up as punishment for not bringing him evidence against Lee? One thing for sure, he wasn't going to follow through with his end of the deal and offer her and Tyler new identities.

She didn't trust him. She couldn't trust anybody.

Except Gray.

Where had that come from?

"Look, if I'm guilty of anything, it's bad judgment," she said. "I'm trying to make up for that. You've got to believe me. You've got to let me try to reach Gray."

He glanced at her, then back at the rearview.

"Can't stop now. I'll get as close to the cave as possible. Grab an LED lamp from the bag so you can see where you're going. It's dark in there. Once you've made it through to the other side of the cave, send the signal, like I showed you."

She dug in his backpack on the floor and found the lamp.

"Protein bars and water," he said. "It's always good to be prepared. For anything."

In other words, in case she found herself alone

in the wilderness. Good, the thought *had* crossed his mind.

She shoved the protein bars and water into her shoulder bag.

"Stick to the right side of the cave. You've got gloves?"

She nodded the affirmative.

"Good. Go slow, watch your step, watch for animals."

"Wonderful."

"They don't like you, either. You should come out on a trail above Bear Lake. Stay hidden in case your husband's camp is close. Gray is probably not far from there. You have a compass?"

She shook her head. "Side pocket. Get it. And the map of the Cascades."

Compass and map in hand, she looked at him.

"The federal agent isn't going to be happy that you've disappeared," he said.

"I'll deal with his suspicions later, once I know Gray is safe."

She could handle anything, even Washburn's ridiculous charges, if she knew Tyler and Gray were out of danger.

"I'm pulling over up there. Get ready. I'll park and distract whoever is behind us. Either it's someone with the forest service, in which case they'll send me back down the mountain, or—" He hesitated. "It's someone else. In either case you move, got it?"

"Yes."

"I really don't like your doing this by yourself."

Katie wasn't thrilled about it, either. But there was no alternative. She wouldn't go back without trying to warn Gray.

Neutralize him, Washburn had ordered.

That could mean tie him up, knock him out or…

No, she couldn't think about it.

"See, over there." He pointed.

She spotted the opening about fifty yards away. He slowed the car, glanced in his mirror and adjusted the knife at his belt.

"I'm sorry for dragging you into this," she said. "If it helps, tell them I ran off on you."

"Don't worry about it. When I stop you need to get down. Open your door and sneak toward the cave. Stay low, use the truck as cover to stay hidden, got it?"

"Yes."

He turned the wheel left, parking at an angle so their pursuer couldn't see her car door.

He flung open his door and got out. Turning, he nodded an encouraging smile, shut his door and approached the other car. Katie slipped out of the truck and crouched down.

"Hello?" he called.

Nothing. Then a shot rang out.

"That was a warning," a voice called back. "Now get the hell out of here."

"A boy's gone missing," Jacob said. "I'm part of the search efforts."

"There's no boy up here. You're trespassing."

Gripping her shoulder bag, Katie raced to the cave, determined to keep going until she came out the other side.

Had she lost her mind? What had Gray told her? Never hike alone in unfamiliar territory?

Yet here she was doing it again.

To save Gray's life.

Male voices echoed behind her. She shut them out, hyperfocused on making it through the cave.

Move. Don't stop; don't think. You're on your own. Good practice for the rest of your life.

She thought about the money she'd put away, enough to live comfortably in a two-bedroom apartment somewhere in the Midwest with her children. She'd done some research, daydreaming about her new life.

Yet only now had it become a reality for her. She thought about raising her son and a baby alone. She'd be sleep-deprived and always looking over her shoulder.

No, she wouldn't live that way. She was smarter than anyone gave her credit for. They'd always called her Cutie Pie Katie. But she was really a smart girl who'd hidden her intelligence so she wouldn't scare off the handsome boy, Lee Anderson.

Yet Gray had never been intimidated by her brains.

Forget it. Gray thought her a drug dealer's whore.

She should have left Dad a note explaining what she was doing. But there hadn't been time and the less he knew, the better. She didn't want it to appear that he was involved in any wrongdoing.

Her new motto: keep people at a distance to protect them. Even new friends she'd make when she and Tyler moved to the Midwest would be nothing more than acquaintances.

She'd become quite good at keeping people away.

Carefully navigating into the cave, she flipped on the mini-LED to guide her. Move quickly, but cautiously, she reminded herself.

A gunshot rang out behind her. A second warning shot?

Her fingers trembled.

Don't panic. You can't help Jacob.

But she could help Gray.

"Keep to the right," she whispered, eyeing the ground to sidestep any protruding rocks. She wondered how deep this cave was and if there was another to follow. Jacob had given her a map but she was sure the inside of the cave wouldn't be on it.

She stumbled on a rock, righted herself and kept going. "I'm an expert hiker," she told herself.

As a kid, she'd loved to hike. Not with her parents, of course, but with her friend Adam.

He'd shown her such wonderful things on their hikes: rare birds, plants, miniwaterfalls created from melting mountain snow. He'd shown her beauty and taught her to listen to her instincts.

You can do anything in the wilderness. It has everything you need.

Adam had said that, convinced her that people could live in the middle of nowhere, surrounded by lakes and wild animals. He made it sound like Shangri-La.

She didn't imagine him speaking to her like that now, and not because he detested her, but because something critical had changed inside of him. He no longer embraced the beauty of nature. He respected it, but kept it at a distance.

She should be close now. Keep going. Stop thinking about the past and your regrets.

Focus on the future.

Find Gray and warn him about Washburn's plan.

Find Tyler.

Disappear.

A silver light glowed from the end of the cave. It was surreal-looking, almost magical. She picked up her pace, using the cave wall for support.

She glanced over her shoulder. Silence echoed

back at her. She hoped Jacob was heading back down, safe and unharmed.

She reached the other end of the cave and her breath caught at the awesome view. The moon reflected off a lake below. Bear Lake? She hoped.

It seemed brighter up here, the air fresher. But she couldn't see the actual campgrounds. Later, she'd go in search of her ex-husband and Tyler after she'd found Gray.

A thought struck her. What if Washburn's man had already neutralized him? She grabbed a can of pepper spray from her bag. It was the only weapon she had since Gray had taken her pistol.

She spied a trail about ten feet away.

"Off of me!" a man cried.

She jumped back toward the cave, scanned the area and clutched the pepper spray.

"God, no, I'm so sorry." It was Gray's voice.

She bolted upright and headed toward the sound. Okay, probably not the smartest idea, but there was something about the ache in his voice that drove her to him. It sounded like…

Surrender.

No, that couldn't be.

She started down the trail and reached a switchback. As she turned, she stopped short at the sight of Gray, standing naked except for his undershorts.

"Gray?"

He turned and studied her as if he didn't recognize her. With arms stretched out at his sides, palms up, he said, "There's blood everywhere. I can't get it off."

What the heck was going on? She had to get him away from the edge of the mountain.

"It's okay," she said. "I can help you."

"I have to go now. I have to find Hoot." He glanced over his shoulder as if he planned to jump.

Her blood chilled. Was he having a breakdown? Suffering from dehydration? Or had Washburn's agent done something to him?

"He's down there." Gray eyed the dark mass below. "I'm coming, Hoot!"

"No, you're wrong," she said, trying to mask the panic strangling her vocal cords. This was no time to lose her nerve. "I saw him up above," she said. "He's taken shelter in a cave for the night. He's waiting for you."

He cocked his head to the side. "A cave?"

"Yes." She motioned with her hand. "Right up there."

"Caves have wild animals."

"Not this one. It's safe. What happened to your clothes?"

He looked down at his body. "Blood, everywhere. On my skin."

This reminded her of the time a kid suffering from hallucinations was brought to the nurse's office at Lakewood High School. It turned out someone had laced his soda with PCP.

Gray had that same faraway, confused look in his eye. He was out of his mind, which meant at any second he could throw himself over the edge.

"Hang on, Hoot!" she called over her shoulder, then glanced back at Gray. "Come on, he's been waiting."

He started toward her.

"Your clothes—"

"No! They're covered in blood."

His jacket, pants and three layers of shirts were scattered across the ground. There was no blood on them.

"Get your backpack," she said.

"Blood on it, too."

"But there's a blanket inside, and I need a blanket." She stepped toward him, anxious about being so close. Would he suddenly lose it and try to take her over the mountain with him?

She reached for the pack. He grabbed her wrist with one hand, and pressed his forefinger to his lips with the other. "Shh. The baby's sleeping," he whispered.

"Okay," she whispered back. But he didn't let go.

He turned her hand upward and kissed her palm. "Shh, baby's sleeping."

God, he was out of his mind.

Then he placed her open palm to her stomach.
He smiled.

And she wanted to cry. She hadn't seen him
smile since she'd found him yesterday.

He glanced beyond her. "I'm coming, Hoot," he
whispered.

He flung his pack over his shoulder and took her
hand. The trail was wide enough for them to walk
side by side, which was a good thing because he
wobbled a bit, as if he'd been drinking.

"I've missed you," he said.

Her heart ached. "I've missed you, too."

"Hoot and I, we were on a vision quest."

"How did it go?" she said.

"Amazing." He stopped. "But he left. I couldn't
find him." Panic edged his voice.

"Up here, not far," she encouraged.

They continued up, past the second switchback,
and she spotted the cave. "See, just up there."

"I see butterflies and stars, and the moon," he
said, sounding like a child.

They approached the cave and he called out,
"Hoot! Hoot, where'd you go?"

A light blinked from the other end of the cave.

"Who the hell's down there?" a voice demanded.

"Damn it." She whipped out of the cave and
pulled Gray beside her.

"Damn it?" Gray repeated, as if shocked she'd
uttered a curse word.

She scanned the area. *Fake it till you make it.* Pretend to be a wilderness guru or you're both dead.

Gray used to talk about places to hide, but where?

"Hoot's playing games with us," she said. "Wanna play?"

"What kind of game?"

"Hide and seek. We need to hide someplace where he won't find us. A hollowed-out tree, what?"

"He knows that one," he huffed with a wave of his hand.

They were minutes away from being discovered and Gray was out of his mind.

"Where can we hide, Adam, where?"

He scanned the area and his eyes widened. He smiled. "There."

He pointed down the side of the mountain.

"Great," she muttered.

He dropped his backpack to the ground and opened it, looking for God knew what.

She let go of his hand and peered into the cave entrance. The light blinked back at her. "Answer me!"

Not good. They could be killed and buried out here and no one would find them. She wished Gray had his senses about him, she wished—

"Follow me," he whispered.

She glanced up to see Gray teetering on the edge of the trail; a cord was tied around his waist and anchored to a tree root that had embedded itself into the mountainside.

"No." She rushed toward him but he fell back and disappeared into the darkness.

She leaned over the edge of the trail and spied into the blackness below. God, she should have protected him, saved him from—

"Ouch." His voice echoed.

"You're okay?"

"Of course I'm okay. I wish I'd worn my boots."

She glanced over her shoulder and spotted the flashlight flickering inside the cave. Their pursuer was closing in and she had no place to go…but down.

She grabbed his backpack, tied it shut and whispered, "Incoming."

She let it drop.

"Ouch. Again."

She pulled on the cord. To think that even in his altered state he'd been able to tie a secure knot. She gripped the rope and slid down, blocking out common sense. What did she think she was doing rappelling down the side of a mountain? But if Gray could make it in his state, she should be able to—

"Let go of the rope," Gray whispered.

Said the man who's temporarily insane.

"I've got you, sweetie."

Yep, certifiable.

His solid hands gripped her waist and she let go

of the rope. They were so close, and he was so naked.

The light flashed above them. "He's going to find us."

"No, he's not," he said, like it was the dumbest thing he'd heard all day. He put his arm around her shoulder and pulled her close. "Look."

A fallen boulder had cut into the side of the mountain, making a small cave, big enough for one or maybe two people.

He took her hand. "Let's go."

"Blanket," she whispered.

"I'm fine."

"I'm freezing," she lied. He may not feel cold in his state but she knew the dangers of hypothermia.

He opened his pack and pulled out the blanket. He wrapped it around her shoulders.

"Show yourselves!" the voice demanded.

Gray led her to the small overhang and motioned for her to climb in first. She did, and he shoved his body up against hers.

Facing her.

"Don't worry," he whispered. "Hoot was the best teacher."

It was dark beneath the overhang and she could barely make out Gray's face, but she could feel his smile. Deep in her chest she felt the smile of that shy boy she used to sneak away with.

"Damn it!" the voice swore from above.

Gray opened his mouth in an *O,* as if he were quite pleased with himself.

"There's no one here, I told you that," another voice said.

"I heard something."

"Let it go already. Come on, I'm hungry and tired."

"If that Robinson guy knows about the cave, maybe he's told someone else."

"He won't tell anyone. I took care of him. Can we please get back to town?"

They'd killed Jacob?

Which meant they'd have no hesitation in killing Gray and Katie.

"We need to destroy the cave, tomorrow."

"With all these cops everywhere?"

"I don't care. We're blowing it up first thing."

"Yeah, yeah. I'm hungry."

"Me, too," Gray said.

"See? You hear that?" one of the men said.

She put her finger to Gray's lips.

This was it. They were going to die, and Tyler would be sentenced to a life of hell with Lee. Unless…

She leaned forward and kissed Gray.

Chapter Nine

"I didn't hear anything," a male voice said from above.

"Quiet," the man ordered.

Katie deepened the kiss, teasing Gray with her tongue in the hopes of keeping him quiet long enough for the guys to lose interest.

"You're hearing things. Let's go," the one guy said.

"Not yet."

Katie placed her hand against Gray's naked chest, hoping her touch would calm him. He moaned against her lips and slid his arm around her lower back to pull her close.

A sob caught in her throat, but not because he was being forceful. She wanted him to touch her, to kiss her.

To want her.

She wanted this hero to accept and love her.

This was an illusion. He'd looked at her with such disappointment today. Yet right now, under the influence of whatever he suffered from, Gray cherished her.

"I want dinner and I've got the car keys," the man said. "Let's go."

"Fine, damn it."

They were leaving. She could stop kissing Gray.

She could, but she didn't. He tasted too good, his tongue gentle as he flirted back, shooting waves of desire across her body.

Lordy, she never thought she'd feel this kind of pull toward a man again, but it was Adam, and he tasted of honor and determination, seasoned with vulnerability. He was desperate to have her.

He was also out of his mind, high on some kind of hallucinogen.

She broke the kiss and noticed he was out of breath.

"That was fun," he said.

Fun? She didn't think he had a word like *fun* in his vocabulary. But then, he wasn't himself.

"Why did you stop?" he asked. "Is Big Bill coming?" He peeked out of the cave.

She scolded herself for taking advantage of him in this state.

He smiled and reached up to stroke her hair. "What is it, Katie May? You want to wait for our

wedding night, don't you, so it's special? I understand."

Katie's heart splintered at his gentle, sweet tone.
He guided her cheek to his naked chest and continued to stroke her hair.

Memories of her wedding night clawed at her. It
hadn't been anything special or extraordinary. She
and Lee had had sex before the wedding, after Lee
convinced her practice would make their wedding
night remarkable. Lying against Gray, she realized
she barely remembered it.

Lee had convinced her of a lot of things back then.
She'd been so trusting, so grateful that someone as
important as Lee Anderson had loved her.

"Sweet Katie May," Gray whispered in a
singsong voice. "Don't worry, I won't let him hurt
you."

"Who?" she said, her heart skipping a beat.

"Big Bill. He's bigger, but I'm smarter. Hoot
taught me… Where is Hoot, anyway?" He started
to edge out of their spot.

"No, don't." She placed her hand to his cheek.
"It's a game, remember? You hide and Hoot will try
to find us? He wants to see how good you've
become at wilderness survival."

"Oh, yeah."

Placing her hand on his chest, she nuzzled
against his shoulder. She couldn't continue their
search for her son with Gray in this condition, and

she couldn't abandon him. She hoped whatever was muddling his brain would move through his system quickly and they could continue their search for Tyler at sunrise. She hoped that her husband and his men were smart enough not to hike in the dark. If Tyler lost his footing—

"Sweet Katie May," Gray whispered again. "I love you so."

She blinked back tears and pulled the wool blanket across them. A few minutes later he started to shiver.

She propped herself up on one elbow and looked at him. "Adam?" He didn't answer, but his teeth chattered.

Hypothermia was one thing he didn't need to be stricken with on top of whatever trip he was on.

"We need to build a fire," she said.

He acted like he didn't hear her. Heck, she didn't know how to build a fire. How long would it take her to figure it out?

"We've got to get you dressed," she said.

She reached for his pack and pulled out an undershirt and wool shirt. "Sit up," she said.

"No," he moaned. "Blood, full of blood."

"Adam, stop."

Then a thought struck. Body heat. But first she needed to put something between them and the cold ground. She opened his pack wider and found a ground pad.

"Move over so I can lay this down."

He rolled over with a moan. If the cold was suddenly affecting him then he might be coming out of his drug-induced hallucinations.

She placed the mat on the ground and wrapped the wool blanket around him. She stripped down to her underpants and pressed her body next to his, front to front.

"How are your hands?"

"C-c-cold."

"Here." She pulled his hands between their bodies.

"Katie," he breathed. "I sh-shouldn't."

"Your hands will warm up quicker."

He nodded and closed his eyes.

She tried not letting his cold hands pressing against her breasts affect her in any way. She needed to distract herself.

"How long ago did you take off your clothes?" she said.

"Don't remember."

"Weren't you cold?"

"Blood, everywhere," he said, a panicked edge to his voice.

"Shh. It's okay. Everything's fine." She wrapped her arms around him, pulling him onto his side.

"You're soft," he said.

"Are you warming up?"

"Really soft," he whispered. "And really pretty."

"Tuck the wool blanket tighter around my back."

He reached outside the blanket and tucked it between her and the ground pad.

"Warm," he whispered against her cheek. "And really pretty."

She wished he'd stop saying that.

"Will you marry me?" he said.

Now what? She didn't want to upset him.

"Sure, when?"

"Tomorrow."

"Next week," she bargained.

"Next week," he repeated. "I'll marry my Katie May."

She closed her eyes. The thought of marrying a hero like Gray, being loved by him, made her ache deep inside. She struggled to shut out the pain, push it down where it could no longer touch her heart.

A few quiet minutes passed. The chill of his skin seemed to fade, his breath was warm and steady against her cheek. His body jerked, as if he were dreaming.

Thank goodness. At least she knew he'd be safe in her arms. She wouldn't have to worry about him running away from her in a psychotic fit.

What the heck happened, anyway? Is that what Washburn meant when he'd ordered his agent to neutralize Gray? Had he drugged him with something and left him vulnerable and helpless in the wild? Bastard.

As she held Gray she thought about everything she was up against: the Feds, her ex-husband, his rivals.

What about Gray? When he awakened and got his senses back he'd be her enemy again.

Couldn't worry about that. She had to catch a couple of hours of sleep to ready herself for the day ahead.

She'd need her strength to find her son and to protect her heart from the man lying beside her. She couldn't afford to trust him. She couldn't trust anyone, especially not herself where Gray was concerned. Because right now, as they lay skin-to-skin, she felt herself drift into a false sense of security.

There was no security in her life, just a desperate need to rescue her son from her ex and disappear.

GRAY'S HEAD ACHED. Not the sharp tightening of altitude sickness, but a dull, clenching pain like he'd consumed a fifth of Stoli. Solo.

But he hadn't numbed himself like that since his tour in Special Ops, when he'd use alcohol to try and forget particularly gruesome assignments.

Not there anymore. Served his time. Didn't earn back his honor, but did his duty.

He wasn't huddled in a cave in some third-world country. He was back in the Pacific Northwest, owned a cabin in the Cascade Mountains.

And a naked woman lay against him, her soft skin warming his body from his chest to his legs. She clung to him like moss on a tree in the rain forest.

Then he realized he was also nearly naked.

What the hell had happened? Who was this female he must have shared a one-nighter with?

No, something was off.

Get hold of your brain, Turner. Think. What was the last thing you remember?

He'd handed off Katie to the Feds and—

Katie. The woman possessively wrapped around him.

"Unbelievable," he whispered, and started to push away from her.

She moaned and instinctively tightened her arms around his neck.

What had he done?

"Katie, wake up," he ordered.

Instead she rubbed her cheek against his chest and breathed a sigh of contentment.

"Katie," he insisted.

"Hmm?"

"Let go."

"What?" She opened her eyes and stared at him. "You're awake. How do you feel?"

"Release me," he said again.

She slipped her arms from his neck and clutched the wool blanket to cover herself. He couldn't help getting a glimpse of her breasts, naked and beautiful, breasts that had warmed his chest a minute ago.

"Where are my clothes?" He scanned the immediate area. He couldn't look at her, didn't want to remember what happened last night. It both sickened and thrilled him. He'd made love to…a criminal?

The love of his teenage life.

"They're probably up there somewhere." She pointed above.

"What? Why?"

"Don't you remember?" She crawled out from the overhang and the wool blanket started to slip.

"Jeez, woman, get dressed," he ordered.

With one arm across her breasts to shield them, she plucked her clothes from the ground.

"Whatever happened last night, I didn't mean it," he said.

With a defeated expression, she tossed him the blanket. "Until you find your clothes."

He wrapped it around his shoulders.

"What *did* happen last night?" he said.

"Nothing."

He turned away and scanned the valley below as she dressed. She said nothing happened, yet he heard regret in her voice.

Damn, why did his head hurt so much?

"What did you do to me?" he said.

"You can turn around." She flung her bag over her shoulder and walked away from him. "We've got to move."

He followed and gripped her arm. When she turned he read pain in her emerald eyes.

"What did I do to you?" he said.

"Some guys are going to blow up the cave. I shouldn't have slept so long. We've got to get out of here and find Tyler."

She picked up her pace, leaving him standing there, bewildered.

He hated the feeling.

"Come on," she ordered, halfway up the switchback.

He grabbed his backpack and started after her. "What happened? I need to know."

"What's the last thing you remember?" she said.

"Tracking your ex-husband."

"Did you know a Federal agent was shadowing you?"

"Tindle..." He remembered something, a guy trailing him, never too close.

"I overheard Agent Washburn order that agent to neutralize you if you got in the way," she said. "I had to get word to you. Jacob Robinson brought me to a secret cave that led up here."

"Jacob? Where is he?"

"I don't know. He probably went back. Someone followed us and ordered him to leave. I couldn't go back. I had to warn you. There, your clothes." She pointed.

Gray glanced twenty feet ahead of them. His clothes, socks, boots, were strewn on the ground like he'd ripped them off in a fever.

"They might be damp. You should find something dry in your pack," she suggested.

She was right, but he hated that she was giving him advice on how to take care of himself.

"I'll keep watch by the cave," she offered.

"Stand right here where I can keep an eye on you."

She crossed her arms over her chest in irritation.

He hadn't meant it that way. He wanted to keep her in his sights so he knew she was safe.

Bull. He felt grounded when she was close.

"That last thing I remember is…" He slipped on his shirt and froze as it was halfway down, struggling to grip the memory against the pain hammering at his head. He felt her pull the shirt down, over his torso.

He found himself staring into her green eyes as flashes of memory played in his mind. "You were hugging me," he said. "You kissed me?"

She adjusted her bag on her shoulder. "I'll explain everything when we get away from the cave."

"What…why are you even here?" he said.

"I told you, to warn you about Agent Tindle."

Gray wasn't buying it. She wouldn't put her life at risk, or her baby's life, to warn Gray. He put on two layers of clothes, then his wool jacket. "Let's go."

He started up the switchback and paused at the entry to the cave. "This it?" he said.

"Yes. Jacob's secret, at least he thought it was. Last night men came looking for us. They heard you."

He turned and motioned for her to continue up the trail. "Heard me what?"

"You were kind of loud."

"Loud?"

"You acted like you were drugged or something."

Right. A crack across his skull followed by a bullet to his shoulder. No, not a bullet. Tindle had nailed him with some kind of tranquilizer.

"We fought," he said. "The agent shot me with some kind of drug. And Hoot—"

He snapped his attention to Katie and she glanced at the trail ahead, as if uneasy.

"It was like night terrors, like some kind of post-trauma thing, all about Hoot."

"When I found you, you were naked except for your boxers. You were ranting about your clothes being covered in blood."

"What else did I say?"

"Nothing worth repeating. Incoherent ramblings."

His guard went up at the thought of having shared personal fears with this woman.

"I was incoherent, but why naked?"

"You wouldn't put clothes on. You said they were covered in blood. You started to shiver and I didn't know how to make a fire. I thought body heat might bring your temperature back to normal."

"Or it could have brought yours down." He stopped and touched her shoulder. "What were you thinking?"

"Save your life."

His hand slipped from her shoulder and she walked ahead of him.

None of this made sense. He'd handed her off to the Feds. He was done with her, never to see her again, not until he found her son and brought him back. Even then he'd hoped he wouldn't have to see her.

Instead, they'd awakened in each other's arms, their bodies entwined and exhausted, like they'd enjoyed a full night of lovemaking.

Sweet Katie May, I love you so.

A knifing pain sliced through his skull and he fell to his knees. Breathe, had to breathe through the pain.

"Gray," she said.

He felt her hand rub his shoulder and her other hand cradle his cheek. She turned his face and the concern in her eyes shocked him.

"I'll get water," she said.

He focused on taking slow, deep breaths. She slipped her hand from his cheek and a rush of wind chilled him to the bone. He hated taking comfort in her touch.

"Here," she said, holding a bottle to his lips. "Drink."

"I can hold the damned thing," he shot back.

She didn't seem offended by his sharp tone. Instead, her brows creased with worry.

He sipped, slowly at first, then tipped the bottle to get more liquid into his system. Whatever he'd been given last night must have dehydrated him.

"Slow down," she urged.

He took two more swallows and brushed at his mouth with his sleeve. "I'm fine. Let's go."

"You sure?"

"Stop fretting." He stood and fought off a wave of dizziness. He wouldn't let this slow him down. "I think I remember seeing campfires from the ridge. That's when I was blindsided."

"What happened to the agent?"

"I—" He paused. Slugging, rolling, punching and… "I don't know."

"I'm glad you're okay."

He glanced at her. "Thanks to you."

She stared straight ahead. "I can't wait to get to Tyler."

"Why?" he said.

"Because I love him," she answered, as if it was the most obvious answer in the world.

"No, why did you come looking for me?"

"You're in danger because of my son. Why wouldn't I help you?"

Because I'm the enemy. The man who'd like nothing more than to put you behind bars with your ex-husband.

Yet a part of Gray didn't want sweet Katie to go to jail. He wanted her to be safe, with her son.

I love you so.

The drugs must still be messing with his head.

"Do you love him?" he blurted out. Yes, still under the influence to ask such a bold question.

"I'd do anything for Tyler."

"I didn't mean your son."

She snapped her gaze to meet his. "If you have to ask, then you've already decided on your answer."

Meaning what? Her cryptic response irritated his throbbing head. She shouldn't be here at all, shouldn't be helping him, giving him water, keeping him warm when he was out of his mind. She could have gone ahead, found her husband and son, abandoned Gray to die of hypothermia.

Instead she'd stayed back and protected him.

"Water?" he said, offering her the bottle.

You owe her something for saving your ass.

A truce could help him figure out what she was

really up to. Keep your friends close and enemies closer, right?

But he was having a hard time believing she was the enemy when she'd just saved his life.

"Thanks." She took the bottle and kept walking.

They hiked another twenty minutes down toward the campground. She stopped short and handed him the bottle as she stared below.

"What?" he said.

"I don't see anyone. Where are they?" She started down the trail, her gait picking up speed with the decline.

"Slow down," he ordered, but she ignored him, slipping and regaining her balance.

He wanted to get to her, steady her so she wouldn't fall on her butt, or worse.

Fall and lose her baby. An innocent in all this.

"Katie!" he called after her.

She kept going, somehow staying on her feet.

"Tyler!" she cried, nearing the bottom of the trail.

Gray followed her, grabbing on to branches to steady himself. The water had helped him regain a bit of strength, but he still struggled against the buzzing in his head.

"Tyler!" She raced into the middle of the campground, exposing herself to the world.

The drug dealers could be hiding in the surrounding area watching for the Feds. He spotted a cold campfire surrounded by empty beer cans. Jerks didn't even clean up their mess.

She fell to her knees and leaned over, clutching her midsection.

"Katie?" He came up beside her and crouched down, his head throbbing. "The baby, is it… Are you okay?"

She shook her head and held up a pocketknife. "His dad gave him this knife. He was here, Tyler was here."

She looked at him with such defeat in her eyes. He kneeled and wrapped his arms around her, holding her close. Anything to wipe that look off her face.

For a second he felt truth in her anguish and believed she just wanted to find her son; that she wasn't involved with her ex-husband's drug business.

"Aw, isn't that sweet?" a male voice said from behind him.

Chapter Ten

Dumb ass. His compassion for this woman made them vulnerable to their enemies.

"Stand up," the man ordered.

They stood and Gray automatically raised his hands.

Agent Tindle pointed a shotgun at Gray's chest. "Got this off one of Anderson's druggies headed back to town. Nice, huh?" He motioned for Katie to step aside.

Gray was going to be executed right here in front of her?

"I would have had them last night, you stupid idiot." Tindle jerked the butt of the shotgun into Gray's gut, and he fell to the dirt.

"No!" Katie cried.

"Back off," Tindle ordered and ripped Gray's firearm from its holster.

"He's the only one who can find them," Katie said.

"I doubt that. Besides, three's a crowd. You and

I are going to have fun looking for that criminal ex-husband of yours."

Gray glared at the guy. If he touched her…

"What, you think you're going to protect her?" Tindle said, as if reading his thoughts.

Gray started to charge, but Tindle turned the shotgun on Katie. Gray froze.

"Military hero, my ass. I can't believe the drugs didn't send you flying over the mountain into pieces."

"I don't die that easy," Gray said.

Tindle delivered a karate kick to Gray's gut. He went down again, determined that this would be the last time.

"I'll report you to Washburn," Katie threatened, blocking his clear shot. "You'll be kicked out of the FBI."

Tindle laughed, not taking his eyes off Gray. "Like I care. I'm not in this for the glory. I'm in it for the money. I'm going to find that bastard husband of yours and demand a nice payment in exchange for your life."

"He'll pay more if you bring him Gray Turner."

"Yeah, why's that?"

"Because he's the one who got him arrested," she said.

What a pile of crap. Would the jerk buy it? It would be easy enough to check, but not out here with minimal cell reception. Everything depended on how much background they'd given Tindle before sending him on this mission.

"I don't believe you," Tindle said.

"Why do you think I went to him for help in the first place?" Katie challenged. "I knew he'd be sympathetic to my cause because he'd helped put Lee in jail. Turner came back to our hometown and found out about Lee's business. Turner has loved me since we were kids and couldn't stand it that I married Lee. Setting Lee up to be arrested was his way of getting back at him."

She was good, Gray thought. That storytelling gift of hers might just keep them alive a few hours longer.

"That's a helluva story, but by the way you're protecting Turner I'm not buying it."

"Why do you think I'm so protective of him?" she said, eyeing Gray. "He's worth a lot of money to me, as well."

Ever so slightly her chin cocked to the left. Although the Feds suspected she was in this business with her husband, Gray knew it wasn't true.

Katie was an innocent. He felt it in his chest.

And she was trying to save his life.

"Think about this," she said to Tindle. "We can use Turner to help us track them faster."

"Why would he help us?"

"Because his choice is help us or die?" She

nudged Gray with her hiking boot. "Come on, help us figure out which way they went."

Just like that, she'd gone from being a panicked mother to acting the drug-dealing accomplice. She'd grown into a strong, determined woman since high school. This version of Katie Meyers didn't need to impress anyone; she wouldn't fall apart at the first sign of trouble.

Gray realized he didn't know her at all.

"You heard her." Tindle encouraged Gray to get up with a kick to his ribs.

Katie winced. She wasn't going to convince this jerk of her loyalty if Tindle caught her doing that. Gray struggled to stand.

"Your hands," the guy ordered.

"I need them to touch the ground when I'm tracking."

"Then we'll tie them in front." With the shotgun aimed at Gray's chest, the guy motioned to Katie. "Search his pack. He's got to have rope in there."

She dug through his pack and pulled out the parachute cord.

"Make it tight," the guy ordered.

Gray kept his gaze trained on his enemy, not wanting to challenge Katie's composure. She was doing a damn good job at playing this out. She tied his wrists tight, probably figuring the guy would check the knot.

He did, smiled at Gray and said, "Okay, hotshot, find them."

Gray scanned the campsite. He hadn't done this type of tracking in years, purposely staying away from it because it reminded him too much of his own failure. Sure, he could rescue hostages based on solid intel, but could he track by solely following his instincts?

You have the gift, Adam. It never leaves you.

It was like the trees were whispering Hoot's voice.

A cluster of footprints caught his eye. He started toward them.

"What?" Tindle said, pointing the shotgun at his chest.

Gray shoved the barrel aside. "Do you want me to do this or not?"

Tindle backed off, looking perturbed that Gray knew something he didn't.

Gray kneeled beside the footprints.

Study the impression of the boot. What is the state of mind of this hiker?

I don't know, Gray thought.

You do know. If you choose to remember.

But remembering meant recalling the pain and the betrayal. He glanced at Katie, who gave him an encouraging nod.

If he didn't remember, she'd never see her child again.

He glanced at the sun. Must be around eleven. Then he glanced back at the ground, touching a footprint.

"Tyler wore Champion tennis shoes?" he asked.

"Yes."

The boy's tracks were in circles, like he'd been chasing something, or maybe trying to stay warm. A few inches away were larger tracks, a group of them. Gray closed his eyes and pictured the scene, Anderson discussing business with his men while his son played games by the campfire.

He stood and went to the fire pit, placing his hand over the darkened coals. Could have been here last night or last week. There was no way to tell.

Every action in the forest affects all living things around it. Look around, what do you see?

Gray opened his eyes and something shiny pierced his vision. "Over there." He went to the object, blocking out all sound, all thought. Crouching, he picked up a small battery, mint condition, then his eye caught on a piece of plastic, the back of an electronic device. A kid's handheld game?

"They were here last night," he said. He glanced at Katie, shooting her a comforting smile. "Tyler is with them."

"Tell us something we don't know." Tindle grabbed the parachute cord that bound Gray's hands and pulled him to his feet. "Let's go. You lead." He shoved Gray toward a trail bordering the campground.

"These things take time. You can't rush it," Gray argued.

"You're full of yourself. Eyes front and center, soldier."

Gray started up the trail, Katie and Tindle behind him. Gray didn't like this position, being the front line with no weapon to defend himself. At this point there wasn't a damned thing he could about it. He had to go along with the game and wait until an opportunity presented itself so he could put the guy down, safely, without risking Katie's life.

Tindle shoved Gray forward and he stumbled, but didn't fall to the ground. It wasn't a bad idea to play weakling, Gray thought. Tindle wouldn't consider Gray a threat and wouldn't expect Gray's attack.

"Big, bad military hero," the guy taunted. "Doesn't look so bad today, does he?"

"Not bad at all," Katie agreed.

If he didn't know better, he'd think she was his enemy. That was her plan: play his enemy and Agent Tindle's ally. He hoped she could pull it off long enough for Gray to get his strength back and take this guy out.

They headed in what Gray guessed was the right direction. Gray sensed the boy's presence, even though he was probably miles ahead of them. He couldn't explain it, but somehow Gray's awareness was sharpening, an awareness he'd used to stay alive in Special Forces.

Only, this felt different. He was reconnecting with something more powerful, something Hoot had taught him.

Probably aftereffects of the drugs.

Focus, breathe, listen.

Gray struggled to concentrate with Katie hiking so close to Tindle. Who knows what the guy would do? He obviously had no integrity, no honor.

Gray would wait until they made camp for the night to strategize their escape. By then the drug should have worked its way through his system. Gray could focus, get clear and listen to what the wilderness was telling him about Katie's son.

GRAY DIDN'T LOOK GOOD, Katie thought. Whenever he'd pause to search the ground for clues, she could almost feel his body ache as he struggled to stand. How could that be? Because they'd made a deep connection since their intimacy last night.

It wasn't intimacy in the sexual sense. It felt stronger, more intense. When she'd played up to Agent Tindle she knew Gray caught on to her plan. She also suspected that Tindle didn't completely trust her.

It worked both ways. After all, the guy was betraying the FBI for money.

"Keep moving," Tindle ordered.

"No." Gray fingered something on the ground.

"No?" Tindle took a threatening step closer.

"Stop it," she said. "What do you plan to do, carry his dead weight the rest of the way?"

"I'm not convinced we need him," Tindle threatened.

"No?" Gray leaned against the mountain. "Fine. You go on, continue on this trail and end up lost and broke."

"I've got a map," Tindle said through clenched teeth.

"Good for you." Gray stared him down. "A map isn't going to tell you which way they went, is it?"

"They're headed north, to Canada."

"If you say so."

They glared at each other.

Katie's heart sank. Had they been chasing the wrong tracks? No, Gray would have corrected them before it was too late, before they fell so far behind they couldn't find Tyler.

"Why did you stop?" she asked.

Gray snapped his attention to her. She steeled herself against the intensity of his eyes. She knew the anger wasn't directed at her.

"These are false tracks." He crouched down and pointed with his hands, still bound together. "A group goes off this way and another goes off in that direction."

"Which way did Anderson go?" Tindle demanded.

Which way did Tyler go?

"As far as I can tell, a group of four guys, wearing Asolo hiking boots, headed up north. The boy and three men doubled back and took that side trail."

"Tyler?" she whispered.

Gray nodded.

She clutched the jacket material above her heart.

"You're lying," Tindle said. "Come on, keep moving."

"I'm telling you, if you're after Anderson, he went that way with the boy."

They faced off, tension arcing between them.

"My husband is the one with the money," she said. "We're wasting our time following the others." Katie started for the side trail.

"Where are you going?" Tindle said. "Get back here."

"Do you want your money or not?"

"You believe this bozo?" He pointed the gun at Gray.

"He's the best at what he does," she said. "Let's go."

Whether Gray was telling the truth or not, she trusted him to do what was in the best interest of her son.

It started to drizzle. As if they needed rain to complicate their situation.

"The sun sets early on this side of the mountain,"

Gray said. "Would be best to find a spot to pitch camp. They aren't going to get very far hiking with a ten-year-old."

She turned away and sighed. Tyler was out there, alone with his father. God, please let her find them before…before—

A shot rang out and Gray lunged at Katie to protect her. Tindle pointed his gun in the direction of the shots.

"We're not alone," Tindle said.

"Brilliant man," Gray whispered into her ear. "Don't assume they're shooting at us," he said to Tindle.

"What else would they be shooting at?"

"Could be hunters. Season's over but up here no one's going to know."

Tindle glanced over his shoulder. "You think I'm stupid?"

Gray didn't answer.

She wanted to smack him. What more could she do to keep him alive? He surely wasn't helping himself.

Gray pushed away from Katie. "Look, no one knows we're coming, right? Why would they be randomly shooting at us?"

Another shot rang out and Gray automatically shielded her. She leaned into him, appreciating his strength.

"Okay, so what do you suggest, G.I. Joe?" Tindle

narrowed his eyes as he searched the area beyond the trail.

"We passed a cluster of spruce a few minutes ago. Let's get back there, camouflage ourselves and keep watch."

"Set an ambush for them. Sounds good. What about Anderson?"

"We've caught his trail. He's going to have a hard time hiking in the rain with a kid. He won't get far ahead of us."

Tindle motioned for Gray to lead. Gray doubled back and Katie followed close behind him, feeling safe near Gray.

They trudged back to the cluster of trees and Gray started to find shelter.

"We'll stay beneath the trees. You sit out here and warn us," Tindle said. What he really meant was that if anyone was to be shot, it would be Gray.

He was the bait.

She and Tindle found a relatively dry spot beneath the trees, while Gray plopped down by the trail, the rain soaking through his jacket. "This is ridiculous," she said. "Let him come under here. We're sunk if he gets sick and can't track."

"You're awfully concerned about him." Tindle eyed her. "I'm starting to wonder if you don't care a little too much about our hero."

She stared him down. "He's going to find my son."

"That's all you care about?"

"Yes."

"Then you won't mind if I tie him to a nearby tree to keep him from running off?"

"Why would I care?"

He shot her a look of disbelief and went to Gray, grabbing the parachute cord that bound his wrists. He secured it around a branch, then crouched down and got in Gray's face. "Big-shot hero."

He shook his head and started back toward Katie. "So, you got any ideas on how to keep warm, cupcake?"

"None." She stood and sauntered away, trying to figure out how to free Gray.

"I do. I'll start with some of this." He pulled a flask from his pack and took a swig.

"You sure that's wise considering someone could be shooting at us?"

"Oh, but they're not shooting at *us* according to our military hero here."

He tipped back the flask and took another swig, then settled beside a tree.

"Here." He offered her the flask.

"No, thanks. You should put that away. You can't defend yourself if you're drunk."

"You'd be surprised what I can do." He winked and patted the ground beside him.

A creepy feeling started at the base of her spine.

"Leave her alone, Tindle," Gray said.

"I don't take orders from you, hero."

Tindle stood and started toward her, an odd smile on his face.

Panic ricocheted through her body. She felt like prey to the tall, lean predator, who suddenly resembled her ex-husband.

He took a few steps toward her and she stepped back. With his hands out he said, "What's the problem?"

"Don't touch me," she said.

"I said leave her alone!" Gray twisted to face them.

"You shut up." He went to Gray and kicked him in the ribs.

"Untie me and try that, tough guy," Gray said through clenched teeth.

Tindle turned back to Katie. "I just want to share a drink with you."

It was the principle of the thing: she said no, he wanted her to say yes. Men like this always got their way. It turned them on to force someone into submission.

"Don't come any closer," she warned, her voice vibrating with fear.

Don't be immobilized by the fear—use it to beat this bastard.

"Katie!" Gray said. "Don't touch her, don't you touch her."

"Shut up or I swear to God, I'll shut you up for

good." Tindle grabbed the shotgun and aimed it at Gray.

Damn it, she was powerless against an armed man twice her size.

Feel the fear—use the fear. The mantra she'd learned in self-defense class.

Tindle turned back to Katie. The look in his eye made her blood pressure spike.

She took a deep breath, her nerve endings buzzing with adrenaline. "I asked you to stay away from me."

He glanced at Gray, then back to Katie. "Oh, I get it. You two have got something going on, don't you?"

"We're friends," she said, opening and closing her fists.

Heel of the palm to the bottom of his nose. Knee to the groin. She imagined it in her head, imagined her victory.

"Here, I'll put the gun down." He leaned it against a tree. "Can't I be your friend?"

Closer, he stepped closer. Even though she'd told him to back off.

"Leave her alone!" Gray called.

Tindle reached out.

The rage that had been eating away at her since that hot summer night exploded in her chest.

Rage, anger, shame.

"Bastard!" She nailed Tindle in the nose. He

stumbled back in shock and she kneed him in the groin. He pitched forward, giving her the chance to make a play for the shotgun. She got her hands on it and he grabbed her by the hair and yanked.

She swung the gun over her shoulder connecting with something, hopefully his skull. He loosened his grip on her hair and she spun around, swinging the shotgun like a professional baseball player trying for a grand slam.

He waved his arms in self-defense. "Stop! Stop or I swear—"

He reached for his knife.

Somewhere in the back of her consciousness she heard Gray call her name.

Tindle flashed his knife.

"Stop or I'll kill…him." Holding the blade, he raised the knife over his shoulder and aimed it at Gray.

She wouldn't let another innocent be used to keep her in line. With a guttural cry, Katie swung the rifle—

And the knife flew out of his hand.

Chapter Eleven

Gray figured he was a goner.

Instead, Tindle lay on the ground, and Katie stood over him, dazed, the shotgun still clutched like a baseball bat.

For a second Gray thought she might keep beating him; instead, she poked at him. Tindle lay motionless, blood oozing from a head wound.

"Katie?" Gray said.

She didn't move. Gray pulled on his bindings. Damn it, he had to get to Tindle and make sure he was out of commission.

He also needed to take Katie in his arms and ease the horror from her eyes.

"Look what I've become," she whispered.

"Katie, don't," Gray said.

She turned and absently started toward him. But instead of untying Gray, she kept walking.

"Katie, where are you going?"

"Have to find Tyler now."

"We'll find him. Untie me so I can make sure Tindle isn't a threat."

Her shoulders sagged. "He's not. I beat him senseless. I beat him." She hesitated. "To death."

"No, he's not dead. I'm sure of it."

She turned back to Tindle with that look in her eye: hatred mixed with shame.

"Look at me," Gray ordered.

She stared at Tindle.

"Katie, please?"

She slowly turned, her white-knuckled fingers clutching the gun.

"Untie me so I can help you find Tyler. Okay?"

"Tyler," she whispered.

He waited, hoping she'd see the compassion in his eyes and take comfort in it.

"We need to find him," she said.

"Yes."

She glanced at him, her eyes red. "You'll help me?"

"I will."

With a nod, she went to him and started to untie his wrists. Her breath caught and he thought she might to burst into tears.

"I can't…can't get it loose," she said.

"Tindle's knife." Gray motioned with a nod to where it had landed inches from him.

She picked it up and studied the shiny blade.

"Hurry, cut me loose."

He didn't want Tindle coming after her, forcing Katie to use the knife in self-defense.

He sensed she'd never lost it like this before, yet she was prepared: heel of the palm to the nose, knee to the groin. Textbook self-defense for women.

She pressed the blade between his skin and the parachute cord, hesitated.

"It's sharp. Just flick it up."

She did, and his wrists came free. He reached for her.

She scrambled back on her butt and pointed the knife at him.

He put out his hands. "I'm not going to hurt you."

His gut burned at the terrified look in her eyes.

"I'm sorry." He paused. "I'm sorry I haven't been more sympathetic about your situation. Come on, Katie, I need to make sure Tindle is out of commission. Keep the knife if it makes you feel safe."

"It does." She glared at him.

He nodded and went to check on the agent. The guy had a steady pulse but was out cold. Good. Gray would bind him and they could get the hell out of here.

Gray knew the gunshots they'd heard earlier couldn't be a good sign. No one was stupid enough to hunt up here this time of year.

He turned to ask her to toss him the parachute cord.

Tindle grabbed him by the throat and yanked him back. They slammed against the hard earth. Gray elbowed Tindle in the ribs to loosen the grip so he could breathe.

"Get off of him!" Katie cried.

Gray nailed Tindle and got free, standing over him. "Stay down."

Instead, Tindle jumped to his feet and charged.

Gray took a step to the right.

And Tindle went sailing over the edge of the trail. Again.

As Gray knew from experience, that didn't mean he was dead. Gray went to the edge and glanced over. Tindle lay sprawled on a rock, a red stain seeping across his torso, his eyes frozen open.

A whimper echoed behind him. Gray turned to find Katie pointing the knife in his direction, the blade trembling with her shaky hand.

"It's okay. He's gone." He put out his hands, not wanting to spook her. "We need to go."

She didn't move, just stared at the spot where Tindle had gone over the edge.

"Katie?"

She snapped her gaze to meet his.

"We need to go. To find Tyler."

Her gaze drifted to her outstretched hand, and the knife clutched between her fingers. She dropped it and took a few steps...toward the edge of the trail.

"Whoa, there." Gray grabbed her by the waist to steady her. "Careful now."

She started to peer down at the fate of Agent Tindle.

"No, don't look down there." He guided her eyes to his. "Look right here. Look at me."

She blinked. "He's…"

"Gone. That's all. Just gone." And with him went Gray's firearm. The guy had shoved it into his belt when he'd disarmed Gray.

"We've got to get a move on before we lose their trail."

"But you said—"

"I was stalling. I didn't want Tindle putting Tyler in danger. I thought once he found your ex-husband, he'd do anything to get money out of him. Maybe even hurt Tyler. I couldn't risk it."

"You couldn't…" Her voice trailed off as she studied his eyes.

"I'm on your side, Katie. I believe you. Please trust me."

"I haven't trusted anyone for a long time."

"I understand."

"Have you? Trusted anyone?"

"No, not much."

"Hoot?" she asked.

"That was a long time ago."

"I'm so sorry. I had no idea—"

"It wasn't your fault. Hell, I could have said something. I didn't."

"Because you were trying to protect me."

Because I loved you.

"I was trying to protect my brother," she said.

"Your brother? I thought you were protecting Lee Anderson?"

"No, I was afraid." Her voice grew distant. "A week before the party, my brother got caught cheating at school. Dad whipped him and said the next time he'd kill him."

"He wouldn't have really—"

"You didn't see him when he was drunk. Mom left because he'd threatened her with his service revolver. I thought he'd kill my brother and he'd go to jail and Mom had already left, and I would be alone and—" She hesitated. "It would be my fault."

"Why would you think that?"

"Because it is, that's all. It's my fault Tyler is out there with his father. Just like it's my fault…"

"What's your fault?"

She grabbed her bag from the ground and swung it over her shoulder. "We should go, right?"

"Yes. Katie?"

She turned to him.

"Thank you."

"Don't, don't thank me. You wouldn't be here if it weren't for me."

"Sure I would. A little boy is missing. Your little boy."

They started up the trail in contemplative silence. Gray felt so damned protective of her. Agent Tindle may no longer be a threat, but there was no telling what else they'd encounter before they were able to rescue her son.

Then what? They'd go their separate ways and he'd never see her again. Just the way it should be.

Even if she wasn't involved in her husband's business that didn't mean he should risk opening himself up to her, especially now when her life depended on Gray keeping his perspective.

That's all it was: he wanted to keep her safe. It wasn't about having loved her as a teenager, or how he ached to make her smile. This was business, not personal.

Yeah, you keep telling yourself that, buddy.

THE WHOLE THING felt like a nightmare Katie couldn't shake. In the end the agent was gone, disappeared down the mountainside after trying to kill Gray.

Her conscience was eating away at her. What more would she do to this military hero to complicate his life?

Sure she needed his help, but she wanted to protect him from the dangers of her life, of running from a drug dealer. Or was she running *to* a drug dealer? Now she was thinking in circles.

She needed sleep. A good hot meal.

She needed her son.

"Let's rest and eat something," Gray said.

"Why?" She eyed him and wondered how he'd managed to read her thoughts.

"I'm hungry?" he offered.

It had been a few hours since they'd stopped for a rest and her stomach had been grumbling in protest.

Gray sat on a fallen tree trunk, took off his pack and dug inside. He pulled out beef jerky, trail mix and a water bottle.

"We're going to have to find some water soon."

He handed her a piece of jerky and she took it, careful not to touch his hand.

The threat from the federal agent had shaken her, deeper than she'd wanted to admit. It felt like Lee's attack all over again, but in slow motion.

"So, besides being a mom, what have you been up to since high school?" he asked.

Small talk was something she didn't expect, not from Gray.

"Substitute teaching," she said, biting off a piece of jerky.

"You're brave."

"Lee never thought so."

"No?"

"He thought it was stupid. 'Why do the dirty work when you're capable of having your own classroom?' he'd say." She glanced at Gray. "I didn't want to work full-time. My favorite was subbing for Miss Lange's kindergarten class."

"She's still at Redmond Elementary?" He leaned back and smiled.

For a brief second she felt normal, like everyone else, chatting it up with a friend in the woods on a clear day.

"She's still there," Katie confirmed.

"Unbelievable."

"She knows I'll follow procedure in her classroom. She always asks for me." Her smiled faded. "Asked."

"Past tense?"

"There wasn't much work after Lee got arrested. Guilt by association and all that. Even Dad had his doubts."

"About your teaching ability? I'll bet you're great with kids."

"No, about my integrity. The question was always in his eyes—why didn't I turn my husband in to the police?"

"And the answer?"

She snapped up to meet his gaze. "Are you asking?"

"I don't think I'm out of line to want to know."

"I guess you're right, after all you've done." She

took a deep breath. "I bargained for a divorce in exchange for my silence."

"So, you didn't turn him in?"

"Nope. Stupid, I know."

"Did you get a good settlement?"

"I was free of him, at least I thought so at the time."

"That doesn't sound stupid."

"It was stupid to think he'd ever be out of my life, not as long as we share a child together."

"You mean children."

She studied the jerky in her hand. "Right, children."

Her cell phone rang from inside Gray's backpack, startling her.

"You never know where you're going to get reception out here." He held it out to her. "If it's your ex-husband—"

"I'll need to be nice to him if we're going to find Tyler."

"Not too nice." He smiled and handed her the phone.

This time their fingers did touch and a spark of awareness shot up her arm.

She opened her phone. "Hello?"

"My favorite wife, sweet Katie."

She shuddered at the sound of Lee's voice.

"I've got someone who's been asking to talk to you."

She held her breath.

"But first," Lee said, "I want you to know I'm flattered that you came all the way out here to find me. I do hope you ditch that friend of yours before we meet. What's his name? Adam Turner?"

"Yes." She glanced at the rugged countryside. Gray had to know it was Lee by the look on her face.

"I have no patience for a military hero stalking me, Kate. You'd better figure out a way to get to me and Tyler on your own."

"I understand."

"Good girl."

She closed her eyes, disgusted by his praise.

"Here's your son."

A few seconds passed. She felt Gray's hand squeeze her shoulder. His touched calmed her.

"Mom?"

"Hi, honey."

"I wanna come home."

"I know."

"Will you come get me?" he whined.

"Give me the phone," her husband ordered from the background. "I thought you'd want to see him one more time before we cross into Canada. Unless, of course, you want to come with us?"

"That's possible."

"Good. Keep to the trail and about four miles north is a deserted gold-mining camp. You'll probably reach it by tomorrow midday. Take your time. I wouldn't want anything to happen to our baby."

She closed her eyes. He knew.

"Come alone, without the military hero. And, Kate…?"

"Yes?"

"I so look forward to seeing you again, to being with you again."

Laughter filled the line, then it went dead. She closed the phone and ambled to the edge of the trail overlooking the valley. Adrenaline pulsed through her body. Tyler and Lee had to be down there in order for the call to come through, right? She'd see him again, soon.

"Well?" Gray asked.

Now what? She turned to him and couldn't bring herself to lie.

"It was Lee. He's with Tyler."

He stood and went to her, rubbing her back.

"Where are they?"

"He wants to meet at a gold-mining camp about four miles north. Midday tomorrow."

He offered her a water bottle. "It's going to be okay."

As Gray studied her, she tried blocking out Lee's words: *I have no patience for a military hero stalking me.*

When Lee lost his patience that meant he'd

destroy something. She couldn't let him destroy Gray.

He deserved better.

She closed her eyes, remembering Gray's frantic drug trip last night, how she'd found him, practically naked, ranting about Hoot, about loving Katie. He hadn't meant it, but still the words, so tender and genuine, warmed a part of her she'd thought dead since her husband had betrayed her.

She cared about Gray too much to put him in danger again. She'd dragged him into this mess, and she'd shove him out of it.

Even if that meant abandoning him to keep him safe.

GRAY KNEW SHE WAS keeping something from him about that phone call. But Katie wasn't talking.

She'd been slower than usual and he asked if she was experiencing muscle cramps.

"No," she'd said and sped up for a few minutes, then fell back into a slow, lethargic pace. Whatever secret she held on to was eating away at her.

Or was she slow because she enjoyed spending time with Gray?

What the hell would make you think that, Turner? Maybe the fact she'd risked her own life, twice now, to save his. She'd even put off her goal of finding her son to stay with Gray last night and make sure he didn't do himself harm while under the influence of the hallucinogen.

Then again it could be as simple as she needed Gray to help find her son.

And then what? Gray had read the determination in her eyes to free herself of Anderson once and for all. If, for some reason, the FBI couldn't put the bastard behind bars what would Katie do to keep herself and her son safe from her ex-husband?

"At least the weather's cooperated," he said, hoping to get her talking.

"Hmm."

Her mind was far away. He wished he could ease that tension creasing her forehead, stroke it away with his fingers while kissing her cheek and telling her it would all be okay.

Whoa, there, chief. You've completely lost your perspective if you're thinking that way.

He couldn't help himself. Ever since she'd attacked Tindle, Gray realized there was another layer to Katie, another side of her that he didn't understand.

But he wanted to.

The sun set over the Cascades and they made camp for the night. He started a small fire to keep warm. Sitting across the fire from him, she looked adorable with her jacket collar turned up and a cap pulled snug over her long blond hair.

"Why did you join the army?" she suddenly asked.

"To get out of Redmond and shoot bad guys." He cracked a half smile.

She stared at the fire.

"Besides, they paid for my education," he said.

"Do you have any regrets?"

"Nah, not really. I learned a lot."

"Like how to shoot bad guys?"

Was she teasing him?

"That, and the fact you can run all you want, but you can't get away from your regret or your shame."

"No, I suppose not." She glanced up and held his gaze. "I am truly sorry. You lost Hoot because of me."

"Actually, I used to think it was my fault because I didn't speak up. But now...I guess I've realized that stuff happens beyond our control. Hoot had a bad heart. Who could have known when they brought him in for questioning that he'd have a heart attack?"

"I never should have accused him of getting us the beer in the first place."

"Look, here's some free advice. Guilt does nothing but destroy you from the inside out. Let it go and move on."

"Says the man who hides out in the mountains." She refocused on the fire.

"Hey, I hide out because I'm antisocial."

She cracked a smile. His chest swelled with pride. He'd done that.

"Besides," he said, "it's magnificent country out here and this is perfect sleeping weather. Cool, but not freezing. We should go to bed."

She glanced at him and he thought he read panic in her eyes.

"So we can get an early start in the morning," he clarified.

"Oh, right."

Now he thought he read disappointment. Damn, he wished he knew what she was thinking, but she kept her thoughts and feelings buried so deep. Except her feelings about how much she loved her son.

He went to her, draping the wool blanket across her shoulders. "Fire should hold for another hour or so."

"Thanks."

Gray went back to his side of the fire and stretched out on his back.

Even with all the tension and danger surrounding them Gray felt more comfortable with Katie than any other human being.

Except, maybe, Hoot.

Listen to your heart, son. Look for the signs.

Gray had turned away from his heart and stopped looking for answers after Hoot's death. He hoped joining the army would purge the guilt from his system, but instead he'd turned his back on his connection to the wilderness.

It never leaves you. Open your eyes, embrace the beauty around you.

Gray opened his eyes to enjoy the stars and found Katie standing over him.

"What is it?" he said.

"Can I sleep with you?"

He opened his arms and she snuggled against his chest, her body shivering.

"Damn, are you cold?"

"No," she said into his jacket.

Was she crying?

"What is it, Katie?"

"Nothing, it's hormones. They make you cry for no reason."

She leaned into his chest and he pulled the blanket over them. He stroked her back, inhaled her sweet scent and decided he'd enjoy this moment and remember it forever.

Gray and Katie, under the stars.

The moment didn't last. He drifted in and out, his usual rhythm of sleep. Then he felt her shift off of him. He started to open his eyes, but reconsidered. He wanted to see what she was up to.

Cracking his eyes open, he spied her digging into his backpack, growing more frustrated when she didn't find what she was looking for. She stopped and he shut his eyes tight in case she looked at him.

Suddenly he felt her reach beside him....

And pickup the shotgun.

Chapter Twelve

Gray let Katie take the shotgun and waited to see what she'd do next. Maybe not a smart move, but he knew in his heart she wasn't planning to shoot him.

This had something to do with her ex-husband's phone call.

Squinting, he watched her grab her bag and sling it over her shoulder. She glanced at Gray, then turned to head up the trail.

Sitting up, he said, "Not even going to leave me a Dear John note?"

She spun around and aimed the shotgun at him.

"Just…just," she stuttered. "Stay here."

He got to his feet, but didn't move toward her. He knew the safety would prevent her from discharging the gun. She didn't control this situation, but she needed to feel in control. If he hoped to get the truth out of her, he couldn't be a threat in any way.

"I need to do this alone."

"I can't allow that, Katie."

"Why not?"

"I'm here to help you find your son."

"Don't." The gun shook as she aimed it at him.

He noticed her finger wasn't even on the trigger.

"Don't be nice to me," she said.

"Why not?" He took a step toward her.

Her eyes registered defeat, despair.

"I'm on your side, remember?" he said.

"No, no one's on my side."

"What's this about?"

"Lee told me to meet him, alone."

"You want to do that?"

"Of course." She cocked her chin up a notch.

After spending nearly two days with her, he knew when she lied.

Okay, she didn't want to meet her husband, but had to, and didn't want to bring Gray along.

"Why take the gun?" he asked.

"For protection."

"Why not take me?"

"You've done enough. Please, let me take the gun and go."

"Can't do that." In two steps he was up against her, the barrel of the gun pressing into his chest.

She stared at his chest, then up into his eyes.

"You need me," he said.

"No, I don't. I need my ex-husband. He's got my son. And…and maybe I do still love him."

Her words clawed at his heart, but only for a second. He realized she was trying to drive him away.

"I don't believe you," Gray said.

"Damn you." Lowering the shotgun, she let it slip from her hand. It hit the ground and she walked away.

"Katie, wait." He caught up to her and grabbed her upper arm, turning her to face him. "Talk to me. I want to help."

"You need to stay away from me. Lee knows about you."

"So what?"

"I can't risk you getting hurt again. I won't do that to you."

"I can take care of myself."

She wrenched free of him. "Last night I found you half-naked about to throw yourself off a cliff. You were out of your mind and vulnerable, and all I could think of was the teenage Adam who I betrayed and hurt and I'm doing it all over again."

Damn, she truly cared about him.

He lost it, and kissed her. He'd been wanting to do that for more than ten years, aching for a physical connection with this woman.

She cared and wanted to leave him behind so he wouldn't be hurt by Anderson's thugs.

She tasted of sunshine and trail mix and her

warmth floated across his cheeks and down, burning its way to his chest. The kiss grew into something stronger, more desperate, and that's when he felt her hands pressing against him.

He broke the kiss and let go of her. "I'm sorry."

She sighed. "I'm not."

"But you were pushing against me."

"It's a natural reaction when a man touches me."

A natural reaction? Images flooded his brain: her violent response when he'd found her on his porch; her defensive attack on Agent Tindle.

Yeah, it was thrilling how he cornered me in my kitchen.

Katie, sweet Katie. No, it couldn't be.

He ripped off my clothes and took me in broad daylight....

"I'll kill him," Gray said. "I swear to God, I'll slit his throat."

"No, stop." She pressed her fingertips to his lips. "This is my problem. I need to deal with it."

"I want him dead." Rage blinded him. How could Anderson have forced himself on Katie, taking her against her will?

Yet hadn't Gray just done that very thing? He stepped away from her. "I'm sorry, I shouldn't have kissed you."

She hugged her midsection. "I understand." She sighed. "Now that you've accepted the truth I wouldn't expect you to want to touch me, either."

"Katie, I—"

"Stop." She shot him a forced smile. "There's no need to explain."

"You think I don't want to touch you because—"

"Because I'm weak and damaged."

He went to her even though she backed away from him. Taking her in his arms, he said, "I think you're a strong, amazing and beautiful woman." He tipped her chin to look into his eyes. "But I'd never want to make you uncomfortable. I kissed you without asking, and the fact that you'd been, well, what Lee did... I'd hate myself if I'd done anything to make you feel threatened or vulnerable in any way."

"Don't be nice to me."

He leaned back and studied her eyes. "Why do you keep saying that?"

"Because I don't deserve it."

"Yes, you do. You're a brave, loving mother who wants to find her child. What have you got to be ashamed about?"

She rubbed her stomach and glanced into his eyes.

"That wasn't your fault," he said.

She pulled away from him. "I don't want to think of the baby as the result of something ugly."

"You won't, sweetheart. You're caring and loving, and this child will feel so lucky to have you as its mother."

A choked laugh escaped her throat. The words Katie had ached to hear. And they were coming from her childhood friend.

Who'd grown into an incredible man. A man she was both falling for and putting in danger.

"You need to go back," she said.

"Can't do that."

"Lee said to get rid of you somehow and if I don't…"

"What? He'll kill me? I'd like to see him try."

"Adam—"

"I'm good at what I do, Katie. I know I haven't shown it much in the past twenty-four hours, but that's because I couldn't identify my enemies from my friends. Now I know who's who. I'm not letting you go into Lee Anderson's camp of drug dealers without backup. That's all there is to it. I'm going to help you, especially now."

"Because you feel sorry for me."

"Because I care about you. If you berate yourself again about the assault, I swear, I'll turn you over my knee."

She couldn't help but smile.

"Katie?"

"Yes?"

"I'm on your side. But I need to know I can trust you."

"Yes, completely."

"Good, then let's make our plan."

IT WOULD BE THEIR LAST night together, Katie realized. Starting tomorrow they'd have to travel separately, Gray keeping to the trees and Katie following the trail.

When it started to drizzle, Gray made a lean-to against a fallen tree using branches, sticks and twigs. He layered moss, leaves and pine needles on top for insulation.

He made a small fire, then crawled into the lean-to and invited her to join him. She didn't hesitate and in minutes she was snuggled against Gray's chest. They decided to get as much sleep as possible to be ready for tomorrow's confrontation.

"All I care about is getting Tyler and disappearing," she whispered.

"We'll find him, sweetheart. We'll find him and bring him home."

Home. Where was that, exactly?

"Will you go back to Redmond?" he asked, again reading her thoughts.

"I don't think so. Truthfully, I'd planned to disappear somewhere."

"He frightens you that much?"

She heard the edge to his voice.

"I want him out of my life. I want a chance to start over."

"Not easy with the Feds on your tail."

"Yeah, the Feds. I'd made a deal with Agent

Washburn. If I brought him information to help put
Lee away he'd give Tyler and me new identities."

"I don't trust that guy," Gray said.

"I figured the deal is off the table anyway, seeing
as I fled his custody."

Gray stroked her cheek with the back of his hand.
"You okay?"

"Yeah."

"You sure? No aches or anything?"

"I'm fine."

She wanted to cry at the caring tone of his voice.
How could this be? How could this honorable man
care about her after all she'd done?

"I'd give a C note to know what you're thinking,"
he whispered against her hair.

"I'm feeling very fortunate." She looked into his
eyes. "That we're friends again."

He shot her an odd, pained smile and guided her
cheek back to his chest. Friends. That's all they
could ever be.

What she wouldn't give for it to be more.

What she wouldn't give for this child growing
inside of her to be Gray's.

"If you get Tyler, but you and I are separated, I
want you to call Luke Dunham," Gray said. "You
can trust him. I'm not sure about anyone else."

"My dad," she offered.

"He's not thinking straight. When you lose your

perspective, you lose your ability to see things clearly."

Kind of like Katie losing her perspective about Gray. He was supposed to be a means to an end: help her find Tyler and she'd be on her way. Yet she kept finding herself fantasizing about seeing him after this was over, introducing him to her son, spending time at his cabin, riding horses and—

"You still have Luke's number?"

His question shocked her back to reality.

"Yes, in my cell phone."

"Good."

"But I won't need it. We won't get separated."

"There are always things we can't control, Katie."

Like the way her heart had opened up to him, even after she'd promised herself she'd never expose that part of herself again to another man.

This wasn't any man, it was Adam Turner, the boy she could have fallen in love with eleven years ago. Her life would have been so different if she'd ended up with Adam.

"It will be okay," he assured her.

"It will be okay when I'm safe with Tyler."

He stroked her hair. "You don't refer to your other child much."

"I can only deal with one thing at a time." She hesitated. "And I'm scared."

He tipped her chin so she looked into his eyes. "Of Anderson?"

"Of this baby. Of my ability to love it like I do Tyler."

"Don't think that way. You're a great mother. You're protective and caring."

"But what will I say about its father? How will I explain…"

"You don't have to. All that matters is that you love the child."

"I will. I do already. I'll be damned if I'll let Lee sully another innocent person's life. This child is going to be raised with unconditional love and understanding."

"That's my girl."

His girl. His words touched her heart, and the look in his eyes made her feel whole.

Gray started to guide her back to his chest, but she leaned forward and kissed him instead. He tasted bittersweet, full of life and hope.

And she wanted more. She needed to connect to him, intimately.

She let her hand slide down his chest, past his belt. That's what she wanted, inside of her. For the first time in years, she wanted to make love to a man. She wanted to make love to Gray.

He broke the kiss and gripped her shoulders, his breathing short and ragged. "Katie, I can't…"

Her heart split in two. Of course not. She was a weak, dirty...

"Right, sorry."

"No, don't go there. This isn't about what happened to you."

She pressed her cheek to his chest and closed her eyes.

"Katie May," he whispered. "I can't protect you if I lose all sense of perspective here. You've got to understand that."

She did, and she didn't. She thought he was being nice, trying to let her down easy and prevent further embarrassment because she'd forced herself on him.

"To that end, tomorrow I'll give you your pistol back, just in case," he said.

Her heart warmed. He trusted her.

"Thanks." She wanted to kiss him again.

"We'd better get some sleep."

She nodded, emotion clogging her throat. She pressed her cheek against his wool jacket and he wrapped his arms around her back. She would enjoy this moment, bask in his compassion and honor.

Because after tomorrow nothing was certain. Nothing but the fact she would not involve Gray in her plan to run away. She wouldn't saddle him with a fugitive and that was certainly one possibility for her future.

She'd be a fugitive on the run with her son and unborn child. There was no place in her life for a man like Gray.

Even if she was falling in love with him.

Chapter Thirteen

Gray did his best to get a few hours of shut-eye. Wasn't easy with Katie shifting against him, enticing him with her scent, with the cute little squeaks she made in her sleep.

They'd gotten an early start and now, a few hours later, they approached the mining camp, Gray keeping to the tree line, out of sight.

He felt better that she was armed, but he warned her that her little .22 was no match for assault rifles. He'd told her only to use it if threatened by a single target. Otherwise, she'd just irritate a bunch of guys with guns.

Taking a deep breath, he calmed his nerves. This was it: his chance to help her rescue her son and disappear.

Gray might never see her again.

No, he wouldn't accept that. He sensed Katie felt the same way. But they couldn't act on those feelings, not until this situation was put to bed.

Put to bed.

He'd nearly given in last night when she'd kissed him. He'd almost lost his willpower and taken her right there in the middle of the wilderness, which would have been so wrong for so many reasons.

Luckily they'd both reined in their desire. Desire he never thought he'd see in Katie Meyers's eyes.

Katie Meyers Anderson. Pregnant by her criminal ex-husband.

Gray hiked with a more purposeful stride. He wasn't sure how he'd stop himself from slitting the guy's throat when he finally confronted him. Damn Lee Anderson for hurting Katie and bringing an innocent child into this mess.

What will I say about its father? Katie had asked with a defeated look in her eyes that made Gray want to hold her close, warm her to her very core so she'd never question her mothering ability again.

He found himself wanting to do many things for her: protect her, make her smile…make love to her.

"Not happening," he muttered.

They approached a clearing overlooking a waterfall and Katie sat on a rock. She glanced over her shoulder as Gray hid behind a tree. She shouldn't do that, shouldn't look for him.

The fact that she did made him smile. She depended on him, needed him.

She took out the trail mix he'd given her. Gray

leaned against a cedar and did the same. The sounds of the wild calmed him, allowing his mind to drift.

Suddenly an image filled his mind, one of Katie and her son sitting on Gray's front porch sipping hot chocolate from Christmas mugs.

Where had that come from?

"Who are you?" she said.

Gray straightened. His fantasy had distracted him and he hadn't sensed danger approach.

"Your husband sent me," a male voice answered.

Gray peered around the tree.

"You're alone?" the guy said.

"That's what Lee wanted."

"I can see why."

Gray held the shotgun in a deadly grip. Not a weapon he could use from this distance without putting Katie at risk.

Pay attention to your surroundings. Listen. Ask questions.

Okay, why would Anderson send someone to check on her? Because he wanted to make sure Gray wasn't with her.

"What happened to your military hero?"

"He's gone," she said.

"Gone? How?"

"I knocked him out while he slept."

The guy laughed. "A little thing like you knocked out a Special Forces pro? I don't believe it."

"Your choice," she said.

He stopped laughing and glanced at the surrounding mountainside. Gray snapped back behind
the tree. He wished he had a rifle instead of a
shotgun. That way he could get off a clear shot.

"If you neutralized a guy like that, then you must
be packing," the guy said. "Hands up so I can frisk
you."

"If you touch me, I'll break your nose," she
threatened.

Gray blinked. Was that his sweet Katie May
who'd uttered that threat? He knew she could do it,
but he really didn't want her to go to that place
again.

"Oh, lady, I can see why you're the perfect match
for Anderson."

Gray sensed Katie's resolve weaken at the offen-
sive compliment.

Hold strong, Katie. I'm here.

"Whatever," the guy said. "If you are packin'
don't shoot me in the back. I'm only the messenger."

"What's the message?" she said.

"Here."

Gray peered around the tree trunk. The guy held
out a slip of paper. *Make him drop it on the ground.
Don't take it from him.*

"I don't bite," the guy joked.

Gray cocked his gun. Deep breaths, don't give
yourself away unless he makes a move on her.

She reached for the slip of paper and the guy grabbed her wrist. Before Gray could react she put the guy down with a knee to his groin.

"Bastard!" she cried. "You're lucky I didn't break your nose first, you ingrate."

Then she glanced at Gray and shook her head for him to back off. He disappeared behind the tree, gripping the shotgun.

"Or do you think a broken nose makes you look sexy?" She started toward him.

"No, stop," he whined. "Sorry, okay?" He moaned, holding his crotch. "I was out of line."

"You bet you were."

Gray loosened his grip on the gun and calmed his breathing. He would have shot the guy to protect her. Without a second's hesitation.

"'Dearest Katie,'" she started, reading aloud from the hand-delivered note. "'Tyler and I will be waiting for you at the Monroe Street Motel on Highway Two. Can't wait to see you.' Was this really worth the pain you're in right now?" she asked the messenger.

The guy grunted.

"Where the hell is the Monroe Street Motel?" she said.

"About three miles up, there's a turnoff. Go right. It will take you to Highway Two. Follow it to the motel."

"I suppose you're my escort?"

"No way. I'm heading back down to check on stuff."

"Good, you go do that. Check on stuff," she mimicked.

She sounded tough, not at all like the Katie he'd held in his arms last night.

Gray peeked around the corner and watched the guy stumble down the trail.

"I hate him! Do you hear me? I hate my ex-husband!"

Gray heard her, but he couldn't expose himself, not until he was sure they were alone. This could be a test.

"Damn it!" she swore and packed her trail mix. She glanced once in his direction, and with a determined clench of her jaw, she continued on.

Gray kept up with her, using the trees as cover. He needed to be invisible to everyone, even Katie. But she knew he was there, always close, ready to step in when needed.

Ready to take care of Katie.

Not only did Katie feel Gray's presence, it was almost as if she could hear his thoughts and encouragement. How was that possible?

The sun drifted lower over the Cascades, just as she found Highway Two. She wondered how long she'd have to walk before she spotted the motel.

How long before she'd hold her son in her arms?

A car slowed and the driver offered to give her a ride. She refused, even though her legs hurt and her mouth was dry. Gray had given her a water bottle, but she'd finished it by the time they'd hit the pavement.

Hell, the driver could be another one of Lee's men, acting the knight in shining armor. She didn't trust anyone. Except Gray.

Highway Two cut through the mountains and she wondered if this was a wild-goose chase. Then she spied a wooden building and picked up her pace. A blue-painted sign read Monroe Street Motel.

She hesitated, wondering what she'd encounter once she got there. How many men would Lee bring with him?

No, it was okay. Gray would handle it and give her the chance to escape with her son.

She glanced over her shoulder and squinted to spot Gray but he'd been nearly invisible since they'd started out this morning. Invisible, yet she could feel him in her heart.

She stepped onto the wooden porch, her heart racing with anticipation. Opening the door to the lobby, she noticed the front counter was unattended. She rang a silver bell, and glanced outside one more time.

"Can I help you?"

Katie turned to find an elderly woman with gray hair smiling back at her.

"Yes, I'm meeting my husband, Lee Anderson?"

"He rented Room Nine. Here's a key." She placed a key on the counter. Katie hesitated, then gently scooped it into her hand.

It would be okay. She'd get Tyler, Gray would restrain Lee and all would be right with the world. Katie would escape and never see Gray again.

There was no other way.

She went outside, marched to Room Nine and knocked. Nothing. She knocked a second time, but couldn't stand to wait one more minute. She used her key and opened the door.

There, on the bed, were Tyler's clothes and box of hair color with a note attached.

She ripped it from the box, her heart sinking to her feet. She opened the note….

My dearest Katie: You're too late.

GRAY HEARD KATIE'S SCREAM of anguish from his spot in the bushes behind the motel. With swift and silent steps, he broke cover and sneaked into the back window of her room.

He found her on the floor cradling a box in her hand. He did a quick search of the bathroom and closet. She was alone.

"Katie?" he whispered, setting down the shotgun and slipping off his pack.

She didn't answer him.

"Katie, sweetheart, what is it?"

He kneeled in front of her and she looked up with defeated green eyes.

"I'm too late." She handed him the note. "I'll never see him again."

Bastard. This was a game, a way to torture her further, to keep her off balance. More like his way of breaking her so that he could dominate her.

"No, Katie, you can't let him get to you."

"He's taken my son!"

"To torture you. Sweetheart, it's no fun if he can't see you broken and desperate. This is all part of his plan. It's not over. I know it isn't."

"I almost believe you," she whispered.

"Believe me. Now, come on, you've been on your feet all day. Lie down, relax."

She didn't speak, but nodded in affirmation.

"Great, good," he said, sounding nervous. He couldn't help it. He was promising her something he couldn't guarantee, but he felt his assumption was correct. Anderson wanted to see her suffer. He wouldn't let it end here.

"Sit. I'll start a shower, okay?"

She nodded again.

Gray shed a few layers of clothing and went to the bathroom. He turned the shower on and glanced at his reflection. He looked alive, not like the empty shell of a soldier that came back to Washington three years ago.

He looked alive because of Katie. He had purpose. He felt...

Love.

"Damn." He splashed water on his face and struggled to regain his focus. He could do this. He could pull it together and protect her even though he was feeling things he definitely shouldn't be feeling. Not now, not when she needed him to be at the top of his game.

"Shower's ready," he said, stepping out of the bathroom. She walked absently past him and shut the bathroom door.

He had to figure out what Anderson was up to. Gray used the motel phone to call Deputy Connor. "Tom, it's Gray Turner. Don't identify me," he said. "Can you talk?"

"A bit. What's going on?"

"I'm not sure. You can't trust anyone, especially not the Feds. What's the word on your end?"

"There's a group of federal agents headed up to Miller's Bridge by the Canadian border."

"Is that where they think Anderson's crossing over?"

"Yes. How's your friend?"

"She's fine. I'll keep her safe."

"The Feds want to question her. They think she's aided and abetted Anderson in getting passports and making arrangements on the other side."

"Trust me, she's not a part of this. She just wants her son back."

"Then apple pie it is," Tom said.

"Agent Washburn just walked in?"

"Ice cream, too. Goodbye, sweetheart." The line went dead.

Gray had what he needed. The Feds were waiting at Miller's Bridge. Growing weed seemed too tame for the determined attention of the FBI.

The bathroom door opened.

"That was Deputy Connor," Gray said, turning to face Katie. His next words caught in his throat. There she stood with only a towel wrapped around her from breasts to thighs. The stuff of a young man's fantasies.

Gray wasn't young anymore. He was a responsible adult and former Special Forces agent who'd made it his goal never to get emotionally involved with another living soul.

Even this enchanting girl.

He turned his back toward her and sat on the bed. He wasn't sure he could control himself with her so naked, so close. Close enough to touch.

Suddenly she stepped into his line of vision.

And dropped the towel.

His mouth went dry.

Her fair, soft skin seemed to glow as if she carried some kind of magical energy. He wanted to touch her, taste her.

Instead, he picked up the towel and offered it to her.

She snatched it from him. "I disgust you that much?"

He stood. "No, Katie, it's not that."

"Then hold me, Adam. I may never see my son again and I need to feel connected to someone."

He gripped her shoulders firmly but gently. "I just spoke with Deputy Connor. Federal agents are waiting at the border. They'll find them, Katie. It's going to be okay."

He kissed her, wanting to wash the defeat from her eyes. Damn Lee Anderson for torturing her like this and making her feel guilty about being a good mother.

Gray wanted to make her forget the darkness, wanted to make her feel cherished and loved.

She deepened the kiss and slid her hands between them, unbuttoning his shirt. Their lips still touching, she pushed his denim shirt off his shoulders to the floor. She tugged his cotton undershirt from his jeans and Gray couldn't hold back the moan of anticipation. Hell, he couldn't hold back the need growing inside of him.

She pulled off his undershirt and pressed against him, skin-to-skin. Her warmth enticed him as he fought to keep his need in check. She broke the kiss and started nuzzling his chest, licking and tasting.

"Katie," he breathed. He didn't know how much

more of this he could take. But he had to be gentle, had to follow her lead.

"Bed," she whispered.

He reached behind her and pulled the covers down, then they collapsed in the sheets, arms and legs tangled in passion.

He'd waited his whole life to make love to this woman.

As they kissed, her flirtatious tongue made him ache to be inside her. Their kiss grew hotter, explosive, setting his body afire with a need that scared the hell out of him.

In one swift motion she undid his belt and jeans, sliding her hands down his hips, beneath his boxers. The feel of her hands on his skin set off a new flash of need.

He grabbed a condom from his wallet, then shucked his jeans. He kissed her again, a moan ripping from his chest as he felt her hands brush between his boxers and his skin. Lower, lower.

His need pressed against her, hard and demanding.

Demanding, like her ex?

He broke the kiss and pushed off of her, flopping onto his back. He struggled to breathe.

"I want you, Katie. I want you so bad...." He turned to her and guided a strand of blond hair from her cheek. "But I don't want to hurt you."

"You won't."

"And I don't want to be the consolation prize."

"Don't say that, don't even think it." She cradled his cheek with her hand. "I need you, Adam. You. The hero of my dreams."

"I'm not—"

She pressed her fingertips to his lips. "I've made my share of mistakes but this is not one of them. Love me, Adam. I need you to love me."

She climbed on top of him and he reached for her breasts, cradling them, teasing them. Her eyes turned dark green as she tipped her head back, enjoying his caresses. Her mouth parted slightly as if she pictured herself tasting him. Then she ran her tongue across her lower lip.

He was going to lose it. He slid the condom on, wanting so desperately to be gentle.

As if she read his thoughts, she positioned herself over him and thrust her hips, taking him fully inside of her. He clenched his jaw, allowing her to guide their lovemaking.

"Adam," she gasped.

He panicked. "Am I hurting the baby?"

"No, it's fine." She thrust her hips, taking him fully inside of her. "I want you so much," she croaked.

He buried himself inside Katie Meyers, holding her hips in place, needing that connection as he'd never needed anything in his life.

She gripped his chest and thrust, her eyes

pinched shut. He edged his hand between their bodies and down to the nest of curls, wanting to send her soaring.

"Oh my," she said, anxious, desperate.

She needed Gray to make love to her. Gray. No one else.

"Katie," he whispered. "Open your eyes."

She did, and he lost himself in the emerald depths.

"Please," she whispered.

He surrendered and filled her with his love, feeling both out of his mind yet centered at the same time.

She cried out and collapsed against him.

He held Katie Meyers in his arms, their bodies still joined.

"Adam," she breathed.

"I love you, Katie," he whispered. "I always have."

Chapter Fourteen

Katie never thought she'd feel this way again.

Again?

She'd never felt so cherished in her life.

As she lay in Gray's arms, comforted by the sound of his beating heart, Katie blinked back a tear of regret. This could never be anything more than right now, a one-night treasure.

If only she'd recognized her true feelings years ago instead of chasing Lee, an illusion of the perfect man she'd hoped would give her the perfect life.

But she couldn't go back, nor could she make this magically work out between she and Adam.

She loved him so much it hurt. "I can't believe you're here, that I'm here with you," she said.

"Having second thoughts?" He trailed his fingers up her naked back.

She propped herself up on an elbow and looked into his eyes. "Not a single one."

"Good." He shot her a mischievous smile.

She'd always remember him this way.

"Why the sad look?" he said.

"Thinking about how you almost got killed in the army."

"Dunham talks too much." He glanced at the ceiling.

"You were so brave," she said, realizing that she'd have to be just as brave to follow through with her plan.

Her plan to protect Gray.

"Had nothing to do with bravery." He glanced at her and cocked a half smile. "I was running away...from guilt."

"Hoot?"

"Yeah."

"I'm so sorry." She buried her face in the pillow beside him.

"No, Katie, stop." He stroked her hair. "Things happen. It's what we do with those things that shape us into who we become."

She turned onto her side and their faces nearly touched. "Does it ever go away, the guilt?"

"Only if you let it go." He caressed her cheek with his thumb. "I've been holding on to mine for a long time. I'm ready to let go. What about you?"

She studied his dark blue eyes, which were filled with hope and integrity.

"It wasn't your fault," he said.

She knew he was referring to Lee's assault.

"Yes, but I have to deal with the consequences."

He reached out and placed his open hand across her belly. "Of having a beautiful child."

"A criminal's child."

"With you as its mother. That's one lucky kid."

"I wish…"

"What?" He tipped her chin so she'd look into his eyes. Then he kissed her. The contact set off a flood of new emotions in her chest. "What do you wish?"

"I wish you were my baby's father."

He leaned back and studied her. She couldn't read his expression.

She held her breath.

"I'm honored," he said.

She wrapped her arms around him, holding him tight, and realized that this was true love.

She also realized that if she loved him, she'd keep him safe, even if that meant…

She squeezed him tighter.

"Hey, you okay?" he said.

"Fantastic," she lied.

For she knew what she had to do. To keep Gray safe she'd have to sacrifice their love and drive him away from these violent men. He wouldn't go willingly, she knew that, and she hated having to deceive him.

But she'd do whatever was necessary to protect the man she loved.

THEY WEREN'T HARD to find. Lee Anderson wasn't all that bright. Then again, Gray's wilderness instincts had sharpened in the last few days, a by-product of his determination to protect Katie.

Katie.

They'd spent the night in each other's arms, whispering, touching, loving.

A part of Gray wished she'd stayed back at the motel, but knew he'd lose that argument so he didn't even try. She needed to see her son as soon as possible.

They'd grabbed breakfast rolls at the motel coffee shop, then headed north toward Miller's Bridge. They walked with determined yet cautious steps. Even though the Feds could arrive before them, there was still a threat of danger. What would Anderson do when he saw Katie with Gray?

Gray had told her in no uncertain terms that he wouldn't allow her to be alone with Anderson, not after what he'd done. Then again, it wasn't a good idea for Gray to be alone with the bastard, either. Gray wasn't sure if he'd be able to control his rage at what Anderson had done to her.

Not good. Gray had to keep it together, shelve his anger in order to keep his head and protect Katie and Tyler.

He looked forward to meeting the boy.

I wish you were my baby's father.

Her confession registered deep in his heart. He

loved Katie, which meant he loved every part of her. And although conceived out of violence, the baby growing inside of her deserved to be loved as the innocent miracle it was.

"What do we do now?" she said, eyeing her ex-husband's camp below.

"We wait," he said, shotgun in hand. "Feds should be here any minute. They'll get things started. When they storm the camp you stay up here, and I'll get Tyler."

She reached out and touched his cheek. The warmth jumbled his thoughts. "You shouldn't do that," he said.

"Why?"

"It messes with my concentration."

"I want you to know how much I appreciate this."

"I know."

A few seconds passed, and an odd sensation crawled up his spine. He scanned the area behind them, but no one was there.

"I'm going to relieve myself behind that tree," she said. "The pregnancy thing. You've got to go all the time."

"I'll come with you."

"No." She placed a hand to his shoulder. "Keep an eye on Tyler for me."

She laid a kiss on him that rocked his equilibrium. He read something odd in her green eyes. Probably the fact they both knew this could be the end of their relationship. She'd do anything to keep her children safe, like disappear.

He wanted to go with her. Life without Katie seemed unimaginable.

She disappeared behind the tree. He found himself shaking his head to regain his focus.

He turned back to the camp. What he wouldn't do for a good reason to splatter buckshot into Anderson's gut.

The kid looked healthy enough, Gray thought, watching Anderson hand the boy something to eat. Tyler looked healthy, but sad. He missed his mom.

But not for long. In the next few hours they'd reunite, leave this ugly mess and start a new life.

Was Gray a part of that equation?

He thought so, but hadn't come out and asked. That would be too bold, too aggressive, and right now Katie needed to feel safe and in charge.

He glanced over his shoulder at the tree. Worry settled in his chest.

"Katie?" he whispered.

Then he heard the cry of a child. He snapped his attention back to the camp just in time to see Katie launch herself into her ex-husband's arms.

Something exploded in Gray's chest and he stood in shock, unable to process what he was seeing.

"Katie, no," he said.

Something cracked against his skull and he went down.

Oh, he'd lost his perspective, all right. He'd fallen so hard for her that he'd probably gotten himself killed.

Because of Katie.

"Anderson's been wantin' to get his hands on you, hero."

SEE THIS. *Believe it. Go back.*

Katie repeated the words in her head as she held on to the grotesque creature that had once been her husband. She hoped Gray would buy this lie, abandon her and save himself. It was the only way.

"My, oh, my, you did miss me," Lee said, squeezing her buttocks.

Nausea rose in her throat. She had to do this. This would save both Gray's life and her son's. She'd lay it on thick with Lee, convince him of her renewed love and beg him to take her with him on his journey. Then, somehow, in the middle of the night, she'd slip away with Tyler.

"Mommy!" Tyler cried, racing up to her.

She let go of Lee and took Tyler in her arms. "I'm here, baby."

"I missed you."

"Missed you, too. It's okay now, we're all together."

"We're all together," Lee said. "Do you mean that?"

Act girl, act like you've never acted before in your life. For Tyler, for Gray.

"Lee, you know there isn't anyone else for me. I've loved you since high school."

I love you, Katie. I always have.

The memory of Gray's words ripped her apart inside. She smiled and choked back a sob.

"You do miss me," Lee said, reaching out to touch her cheek. She closed her eyes and leaned into his touch pretending it was Gray.

She opened her eyes. Lee shot her a smile, but she couldn't read it, couldn't tell if he was testing her or if he believed her. One thing she knew for sure: Lee was under the influence of something.

"Look what we found!"

She spun around at the sound of a man's voice. With an arm protectively around Tyler's shoulder, she watched two men drag Gray's limp body into camp and drop him on the ground at Lee's feet.

Swallowing back her anguish, Katie clenched her jaw. Damn it, why didn't he leave?

"I thought I told you to come alone," Lee said, eyeing her.

"Unbelievable!" she cried, pacing around the campfire. "I thought I'd lost him."

"Really?" He gripped her upper arm and she struggled not to wince, for fear she'd upset Tyler.

"The guy is a tracker. He's got a lot more experience than I do." She wrenched free of him and paced to Gray's lifeless body.

Dead? No, he didn't die that easy.

And she'd fight to keep him alive.

"I tied him up at the motel and left him," she said.

"The motel?" Lee raised a brow.

Damn it, think fast, girl.

"What, you think I'd get the upper hand if he was conscious? I waited until he was asleep."

"Hmm. In other words you—"

"Stop. Not in front of Tyler." Katie went to her son and kneeled in front of him. "Can you give Mommy and Daddy a few minutes alone?"

The boy looked at his father with fear in his eyes.

"Go on," Lee said, motioning for one of his men to take the boy away.

Once gone, Lee turned to her. "You screwed Turner?"

If Lee knew that, he'd kill Gray for sure.

"Don't be ridiculous." She paced to Gray's body and back to Lee. "He's impossible to get rid of. The FBI agent couldn't do it, and neither could the bounty hunter."

"Bounty hunter?"

"He was hired by a rival drug gang."

"No, that can't be right."

Gray moaned and struggled to sit up.

"Ah, our military hero awakens," Lee said.

Katie couldn't look at Gray.

"You're quite a pain in the ass." Lee motioned for his guys to pick him up. They held him by the arms and Lee slugged Gray in the stomach.

"This is the pathetic kid that always had a crush on my wife." He smiled at Katie, then delivered another blow to Gray's stomach.

If the FBI didn't show up soon, Lee would kill Gray.

"I'm bored with this. Give me a gun," Lee ordered.

Panic squeezed her heart.

Be strong. Save him.

One of his men handed him a pistol.

"Lee, don't be stupid."

He turned to her. "Excuse me?"

"That's always been your problem, you never use your head." She crossed her arms over her chest.

"Oh, do tell." He stepped toward her, but she didn't back down.

"Gray has contacts with law enforcement. We could make him call in, say he hasn't found you and ask for their position. It's perfect! We'll know exactly where they are and avoid confrontation. Secondly, if they do find us, we could use him as a bargaining chip. He's a military hero, he's got to be worth something, right?"

She framed Lee's cheeks with her hands. "Use everything and everyone around you to your advantage, isn't that what you always said? Well, use him."

His brows knit together as he struggled to discern the truth to her words. "I can't believe this is my perfect little wife speaking to me."

"Ex-wife," she corrected.

He narrowed his eyes at her.

"They say sex is better with the ex." She winked.

Gray moaned and a piece of her heart seemed to break off.

He'd never understand. Never forgive her.

Didn't matter, not if this kept him alive.

"I had a signal yesterday, I wonder if…" She pulled out her phone.

Lee snatched it from her. "We have our own, more sophisticated equipment."

"Good, have him call."

Lee eyed her with suspicion.

"Come on, Lee, we're better off if we know where they are."

"My wife!" he said with pride to his men, then turned his attention to Gray. "Stand him up."

Two men pulled him up. Katie ground her teeth at the sight of the bruise forming above his eye.

Lee went to Gray and shoved some kind of walkie-talkie at him. "If you give away our location, I will kill you. Slowly. Painfully." He tapped the tip of the gun barrel to Gray's head and smiled. "Do it."

Gray punched in a number. Then he looked at Katie.

The hatred in his eyes burned a hole through her heart.

"Tom? It's Gray. We're still south of Miller's Bridge. Ran into some problems."

Lee smacked Gray in the head with the barrel of the gun.

Gray closed his eyes against the pain.

"No, it's the woman," Gray said. "She wasn't feeling well so we took a break. Where are you? Uh-huh. Definitely not. Okay, I'll check in later. Katie is anxious. Yep…nope…talk to you later."

Lee ripped the phone from his hand. "Where are they?"

"Monroe Street Motel. They think you're crossing the line with something more serious than pot. They sound motivated to find you."

Lee paced to the campfire.

Katie held her breath. Would he decide Gray had served his purpose and kill him?

"We'll split up," Lee announced. "Throw them off track."

"What about the meet over the border?" one of his men questioned.

"We'll make it. Pack up camp. You two, take the military hero and my son around the eastern side and the rest of us will take the western trail. We'll meet you at Miller's Bridge."

"Wouldn't it make more sense to keep Tyler with us?" Katie asked.

Lee ignored her and glanced at his men. "Make sure our hero and the boy are in front. That way the Feds will see them and won't shoot."

"Lee!" Katie protested.

"No one's going to shoot a kid, Katie. Don't be stupid."

She clenched her fists. He wasn't thinking straight.

Tyler's only chance was Gray.

She glanced at him. He hadn't taken his hateful eyes off of her.

She knew no matter how broken he was, honor coursed through him. He would protect an innocent child.

"I need to speak with Tyler before we go," she said as controlled as possible.

"Quick," Lee ordered. "We don't have much time."

"Aren't you going to say goodbye?"

Lee ignored her, turned and ordered his men to bind Gray's wrists. She ripped her gaze from the scene.

She walked toward a tent where one of Lee's men had taken Tyler. She would be strong for her son, strong and smart.

"Hey buddy," she said, climbing into the tent. "You can go," she said to the man.

"I take orders from Anderson."

"Funny, that's my last name, too. Go on, he needs your help packing up."

The guy shrugged and left the tent. She took Tyler's little hands in hers and smiled. "I love you so much, baby."

"What's going on?" His green eyes radiated panic.

"Your dad, he's…"

"He's crazy, isn't he?"

"Why do you say that, honey?"

"He yells at me, then he tells me he loves me then he dyes my hair orange, then makes me hike in the rain, without a coat!"

"I know, baby. He's…sick, kind of. Tyler, listen to me. I need you to be a big boy right now. Can you do that?"

"I want to be with you."

Her heart ached. "I know, honey. And you will be. But right now, I need you to do as I say, okay? We're splitting up temporarily and you'll be with some men. One of them is Gray, the man they brought into camp just now."

"He looks mean."

She could see why he'd think that, considering the way he'd been looking at Katie.

"He's upset, with me. I did something very bad and I can't take it back."

"Say you're sorry."

"That won't work, baby. But I care about him, a lot. I need you to stay close and take care of him. Can you do that?"

"I guess." He glanced at their hands.

"I found this." She handed him his pocketknife.

He wouldn't take it.

"Tyler, I need you to take it to help my friend Gray."

He looked at her in question.

She squeezed his hands. "Your father said I babied you, but I disagree. I think you're growing into a fine young man. I need you to promise me you'll take care of yourself and Gray. He's a very smart man and knows things about the wilderness. He knows how to find people. Once this is all over, you can ask him to find me, okay?"

"Can he do that?"

"Yes, and he will, you know why?"

He shook his head.

She smiled and hugged him. "Because he's a real hero, baby. He's my hero and I'll love him forever."

Chapter Fifteen

Gray hoped Deputy Connor understood his cryptic message. When Connor had asked if everything was okay, Grey had answered definitely not.

Gray had had his heart ripped from his chest. Only this time it was worse. This time he loved with a man's heart, not a boy's infatuation.

Gray had fallen hard for a woman who was using him.

Again.

Had it all been a manipulation?

As they headed west, he didn't bother telling his captors they should make camp before they lost light. Why make their jobs easier? Just keep your mouth shut.

And feel your heart bleed into your chest.

Fool.

A few minutes later the big guy stopped. "We'll camp here for the night."

One of the other three men, a skinny, young guy, grabbed him from behind and shoved him shoulder-first into a boulder. Gray slid down beside it.

"You should make him pitch the tent," the skinny guy said.

They were going to pitch a tent out here? With this wind, it would blow away in seconds. Again, not his problem. He wanted to get back to his normal, mundane life.

"Sit there and be quiet," the big one ordered.

Gray hadn't spoken since they'd split up from Anderson.

"Come on, kid." The guy motioned for Tyler. The boy glanced at Gray and smiled.

Like mother like son, the kid had a charm about him.

"He doesn't look that tough. I say untie him and make him pitch the tent," the thin man argued.

"A tent won't stay up in this weather," Gray offered.

"Shut up," the other threatened. "Tie him to that tree over there."

"Isn't he sleeping in the tent?" Tyler asked.

"Nah, kid, he's dangerous."

The skinny guy and a third, quiet man wearing a baseball cap led Gray to a nearby tree and strapped his already-bound wrists to the trunk.

"This should hold him." The thin man back-handed Gray across the cheek.

Gray waited for the rage to rise up and explode from his chest. Instead, he felt nothing.

Katie had been using him all along.

Eight years in the service hadn't taught him much about people. He hadn't learned to protect himself emotionally.

He leaned against the tree trunk and watched the bozos try to pitch the tent in this wind tunnel. He would have laughed at their incompetence, but didn't want to taunt the idiots. They had the guns, after all.

He closed his eyes, which was a mistake since the image of Katie's sparkling green eyes taunted him. Hell.

A few minutes passed, he wasn't sure how long. He didn't care. He was stuck in his own hell.

Listen with your heart.

Hoot's voice haunted him.

"Give it up, old man," Gray whispered. "The heart's broken."

GRAY DRIFTED IN AND OUT of consciousness, and each time he awakened a fresh arc of pain sliced through his chest. No, he had to fight this, had to...

"You thirsty?"

He opened his eyes. Tyler was kneeling beside him holding a bottle.

"It's okay, it's just water," the boy said.

"Go away, kid." He glanced at the group around the campfire.

"They don't know I'm here," he said. "They're drinking whiskey or something."

"Doesn't matter. Get away from me."

The boy blinked, twice. Then he held the water bottle to Gray's lips.

"Don't you understand English?" Gray said.

"I understand English, and Spanish and some French."

"Then go away. Go on, get."

"I'm not a dog. Sheesh."

"My dog takes orders better than you."

"I take orders." He put down the bottle.

Good, he was going to leave Gray alone and take those innocent green eyes with him.

Katie's eyes.

Tyler pulled a bag of trail mix from his jacket. "You hungry?"

"Thought you said you take orders."

The kid sat back on his knees and studied Gray. "I take orders from one person only. My mom."

Gray looked away.

"She told me to take care of you so that's what I'm doing."

Guilt, Gray thought. A great motivator.

"I'll be fine, kid. I don't need your help."

"I'm going to need your help to find my mom."

Gray stared him down. "She doesn't want to be found, remember? She's gone off with your dad."

"She said you'd find her, that you were smart and you know how to track people."

"Why would I want to find her?"

"Because, she said you're a hero. She said you're *her* hero."

"She was wrong."

"She's never wrong. She's my mom."

Gray wanted to shoot back a smart-aleck comment, but the love in the kid's eyes stopped him cold.

"Besides…" Tyler hesitated and fiddled with the bag of trail mix. "She said she loves you."

The wind ripped from Gray's chest.

"You've got to find her before my dad hurts her again," Tyler pleaded.

"Hey, kid, get away from him," the big guy ordered, walking toward them. He grabbed Tyler by the arm and pulled him back to the group. "Stay away from the prisoner. He's a bad guy."

Tyler glanced over his shoulder at Gray.

She said she loves you.

The fog of betrayal parted and he could hardly breathe. She loved Gray? But why did she launch herself into Lee Anderson's arms?

Because she thought that would drive you away. Because she doesn't want to put you in danger.

When Anderson demanded the gun to shoot

Gray, she'd called her ex-husband stupid. That could have gotten her killed. But she'd risked it.

To keep Gray alive.

Son of a bitch.

He'd been blindsided by an old wound: betrayal. A wound that he'd never fully recovered from. And now Katie was with that bastard Anderson, sacrificing herself to keep Gray and Tyler safe.

"I'm coming, Katie. I'm coming," he whispered.

He wasn't sure how, but he'd get away from these jerks, find her and get her and Tyler to safety.

But could she ever forgive him for being so blind and not trusting in their love?

LIKE HIS MOM, Tyler ignored Gray's words and listened with his heart. Thank God.

The boy returned in the middle of the night and used the pocketknife his father had given him to cut Gray loose.

Gray tied up the three goons with minimal resistance, which was good: he didn't want to upset the kid. He took the communications device, and he and Tyler slipped away in the night, moving quietly, almost like they'd practiced this before.

But this was the first time Gray hiked with Katie's little boy. He was a natural, and Gray enjoyed his company.

Gray called in and found out when and where

the Feds were going to move in. Gray needed to be there to make sure Katie wasn't hurt.

First he had to get Tyler safe. They waited at the rendezvous by Harper Falls. The plan was for a team to pick up the boy and Gray, take them to safety, then a second team would continue north to Miller's Bridge and arrest Anderson and his men.

Screw safety. Gray needed to get to Katie.

"I want to come with you to rescue Mom," Tyler said.

"Sorry, bud, can't do that. This is dangerous stuff."

"Tell me about it. I've been with my drug-dealing father for the past week."

Gray squeezed the kid's shoulder. "I'll bet that was pretty bad."

"He's a complete jerk."

"Can't argue with you there."

A minivan pulled up to the Harper Falls lookout and the door opened. Agent Washburn got out, an assault rifle in hand.

Tyler clung to Gray.

"It's okay," Gray said.

For a second he wasn't sure. Then Deputy Connor got out.

"Mr. Turner," Washburn greeted. "We weren't sure if this was for real or a setup." He lowered his rifle. A second minivan pulled up behind them. He spoke low into a radio on his shoulder, then turned back to Gray. "We're headed up to Miller's Bridge. You and the boy go back with Deputy Connor. Thanks for your help."

"Sorry, sir, but I can't do that. I gave my word to this boy that I'd help rescue his mother."

"Rescue?"

Washburn obviously still thought Katie guilty. Another reason for Gray to be there when this went down.

"You sure you're up to it?" Washburn said, motioning to the bump on Gray's head.

"Never better." He turned to Tyler. "You be good and tell Deputy Connor everything you know about your dad, okay, chief?"

"Find my mom."

"Deal." They shook hands.

Gray got into the van and they started up the winding road toward Miller's Bridge.

"Smart thinking, alerting Deputy Connor," Washburn said.

"Thank you, sir," Gray said.

He eyed the two other guys in the back, both carrying assault rifles.

"Can't wait to put this couple behind bars," Washburn said.

"She's not involved, sir."

"Oh, she's involved. She came to me and said she wanted to help nail her husband. Now she's run off with him."

The only thing Katie was involved in was fighting for her freedom. Gray didn't trust Washburn with Katie's safety.

"I could use a firearm," Gray said.

"Sorry, we didn't bring spares. I'd rather you stay in the van, anyway, let the pros handle it."

Gray bit back a sarcastic remark.

About a half hour later the van slowed and the driver turned off his lights. Adrenaline coursed through Gray's body. He realized that if the Feds thought Katie was a part of the drug business they wouldn't hesitate to take her out.

They parked and Washburn said, "Stay here."

The three men disappeared into the darkness and Gray counted to ten before following. The noise these guys made would alert a bear in hibernation. Why didn't the government send a more proficient team?

Darkness surrounded him, the stars winking from the midnight sky. Damn, where was she?

Stop. Listen. Breathe.

Although Gray had been running from his shame of betraying Hoot, it was Hoot's wisdom that kept him alive during the brutal missions in the army.

Falling to his knees, Gray put his hands on his thighs. With a deep breath he tipped his face to the sky and listened with his heart.

Gray sensed her vibration originating from beyond a cluster of spruce trees to the right. He silently followed it and heard voices echo beyond the trees. He struggled to hear Katie's sweet voice and feel her presence.

"He's back in the van," Washburn said.

"Go kill that bastard once and for all," Anderson ordered.

One of Washburn's agents started back for the van, which meant...

Washburn was on Anderson's payroll? Hell.

Gray waited and snared the agent, putting him down with a sleeper hold. He did the same to one of Anderson's agents, who was roaming the perimeter of their rendezvous.

"You might want to kill her, too," Washburn added.

"My loving ex-wife?"

Gray peered through the branches and spied Anderson put his arm around Katie.

"Your loving ex-wife made a deal with me to set you up."

Gray closed in.

"No kidding?" Anderson backhanded her across the cheek and Katie slammed into the dirt.

Gray wanted to rip the guy's heart out through his throat.

Not yet, he couldn't expose himself yet, but he wouldn't sit here and watch her take a beating. He tossed a rock at a nearby boulder to draw attention.

Squinting into the darkness, Anderson ordered, "Check it out."

Okay, Anderson was down to one thug plus Washburn and his remaining agent. Anderson's man ambled into a cluster of trees and Gray made a wren call to draw him in. Closer, closer.

Gray came at him from behind and put him down with a chokehold.

Down to one soldier plus Anderson and Washburn.

Gray closed in.

"What have you got for me?" Washburn said.

"Money, money and money," Anderson said. "But we have to sell product to the Canadians first."

"Where is it?"

"Safe." Anderson tapped his waist pack.

"You expect me to believe it's in there?"

Anderson laughed. "It's a concentrate, Fed man. That's why it's so easy to smuggle."

Washburn *was* involved in this dirty business. Big-time.

Think. Strategize. If Gray shot an FBI agent, who would believe his story? He could go to prison. He had to neutralize them without killing them.

"What about the woman?" Washburn said.

"You mean my whore?" Anderson smiled at her. "She knows too much."

"So, shoot her," Anderson said casually.

Gray charged the camp, tackled Washburn before

he could get a shot off and ripped the machine gun from his hands.

Gray spun to aim the gun at Anderson and froze.

With a delighted grin on his face, Anderson held a gun to Katie's temple.

"Still in love with her, you stupid punk?" Anderson said.

"Let her go," Gray ordered.

Anderson fired a shot into the sky. "Put it down, hero!"

"You'd take a mother away from her son?" he challenged.

"Oh, I wouldn't. You would."

Katie glanced at him, her eyes wide and pleading.

Gray released the weapon, laid it on the ground by his feet and put his hands up. He wouldn't live through this, but he couldn't live knowing he'd caused her death.

"Kill him!" Washburn said, getting to his feet. He grabbed a machine gun from the ground and aimed it at Gray.

A shot rang out and Gray ducked, but wasn't hit. Washburn fell to his knees, gripping his side. "The bitch shot me."

Anderson kicked the pink-lady pistol from Katie's hand.

"Outstanding," Anderson said. "You've shot a

federal agent. You'll spend more time in jail than I will."

"Damn it, Anderson," Washburn spat. "Kill them."

"Good idea."

Gray smiled at Katie, wanting the last thing she saw on this earth to be the love in his eyes.

Anderson raised the gun, pointed...

And shot Washburn and his agent. Gray went to Katie and shielded her with his body.

"Get off of my wife!" Anderson cried. He was completely out of his mind.

"Move," Anderson ordered, kicking Gray in the ribs.

He got off Katie and stood.

"A sad story of misplaced loyalty," Anderson said. "You tried to save the woman who was a drug dealer with her husband. You went as far as to kill federal agents. The husband gets away, flees into Canada with his wife, leaving you behind to serve prison time."

He extended his hand to Katie. She glared at it.

"Katie, you were pretending all along? You lied about all of it?"

Katie stood and brushed off her jeans. "I didn't lie about everything. I *am* pregnant."

"What, you're pregnant by him?" He pointed the gun at Gray.

"Of course not. I just hooked up with him three days ago."

"Hooked up? She's hooked up!" he cried to the heavens. The man was definitely high on whatever drug he'd created.

"I gave you everything, Katie. I loved you!"

"No, Lee, you owned me. Not anymore."

"I have the gun!"

"I don't care."

"Oh, you will, bitch, you will."

He pointed the gun at Gray's chest.

"Lee, no!" Katie charged, knocking his arm.

The gun went off, missing its mark. What in the blazes was she thinking getting between her ex-husband's gun and Gray? Gray couldn't stand it if she was hurt trying to protect him.

He started toward them and another shot rang out. Gray ducked.

"No more!" Katie cried, kneeing Anderson in the groin.

He doubled over, but still clutched the pistol. "I can't believe you did that," Anderson grunted, then aimed the gun at Gray. Katie tackled him, knocking the gun from his hand.

Gray dove to grab it as Katie struggled with her ex. He heard the grunts of two people fighting for control, but Gray focused on getting his hands on the firearm that would give him and Katie the advantage.

"No!" she cried.

He looked up in time to see Katie and Lee slip over the edge and disappear into the ravine below.

"Katie!" Gray called, fighting the panic in his chest.

He couldn't lose her now, not now, not after they'd rediscovered each other and had fallen in love.

Scrambling to the edge, Gray peered down. "Katie?"

His desperate voice echoed back at him.

Shoving the pistol into the waistband of his jeans, he climbed down the steep drop, gripping tree branches to control his momentum.

She had to be okay. He wouldn't accept the alternative. They'd waited a long time to find each other.

And they deserved to be happy. Together.

When he reached the bottom he spotted Katie lying beside the water on her back.

"No," he muttered, going to her, trailing muddied blond waves from her face. "Katie, open your eyes."

She didn't move. But she had a pulse.

"Katie May. No, sweetheart, no." Gray held her to his chest. "Sweet God, you can't do this to me."

"Gray Turner!" a man called from above. "Turner, it's Deputy Connor. Where are you?"

"Down here!" he called. "I need a medic, I need—"

"Gray," she whispered.

He looked into her eyes. "Shh, Katie, I'm here."

"Is Lee…"

He glanced at her ex-husband's body, sprawled across the embankment, his eyes fixed in a dead man's stare.

"He's gone," Gray said.

She closed her eyes and let out a deep sigh.

Panic fisted in his gut. "Katie?"

She opened her eyes and smiled. "I'm okay."

But he felt the warmth of blood seep out from her body onto his hands.

"I love you, Katie," he said.

"I'm glad."

And she closed her eyes.

Chapter Sixteen

Gray led Maverick into the barn and dismounted. He wished he could have called it a peaceful ride, but he'd be lying to himself. There'd been no peace since the day he'd left Katie at the hospital a month ago.

He'd done the right thing, left her to recover on her own with her family close by. Gray had called his buddy Luke Dunham to check on things, to make sure her family was taking care of her.

Gray sure as hell had failed miserably in that department. A true hero would have protected her. Instead, she'd risked her life to save Gray and lost her baby in the process. Even though it was Anderson's child, Gray knew how much Katie had loved it.

She should have put herself first, but then love makes people do crazy things.

Did she still love him? He wasn't sure so he'd kept his distance, not wanting to crowd or confuse her.

Gray slid the saddle off Maverick's back. It was best this way: one man, one horse and one dog.

Suddenly, Squirt started up his frantic barking. There must be a pika outside the window. No, that was a different kind of bark.

Gray went to the barn door. The wind ripped from his chest at the sight of Katie and Tyler standing on his porch. Leaning on a crutch, Katie tapped at the window. "Hey, buddy, where's your master?"

Before he knew he'd taken a step, Gray was halfway to the cabin.

"Katie?" he breathed her name.

She turned to him and smiled. Emotion gripped his chest. She looked beautiful with her hair loose across her shoulders, wearing a new purple hat.

"Okay, before you have the cops arrest us for trespassing, I tried to call, but your phone's not working," she said.

"Wind knocked the lines down last week." He could barely get the words out.

"How do you get Xbox live?" Tyler asked.

Gray eyed the boy, who looked older somehow. "There's no Xbox out here, buddy."

"No Xbox—what do you do for fun?"

Gray smiled. "I read, make wood carvings."

"Read? Ack."

"I ride horses," Gray offered, wanting to please the kid.

"Cool."

"And, he's got the coolest dog," Katie said. "Could Tyler meet Squirt?"

Gray nodded, his heart pounding. Did he dare hope?

Gray opened the cabin and motioned for Katie and Tyler to go inside.

"Go on in, Tyler," Katie said. "I need to talk to Gray for a sec."

"Squirt, behave," Gray ordered. "He knows basic commands like sit, stay, fetch."

"Awesome!"

Katie shut the door on her son and hobbled to the edge of the porch.

Hobbled. Another reminder of his failure.

"I've missed you," she said.

Gray didn't respond at first.

"I'm sorry I didn't call," he said.

"Your phone's out," she offered.

"There's that. And I thought maybe you needed some space." He paused. "To sort things out."

"What things?" She turned.

Her green eyes captivated him.

"Losing the baby," he said. "I thought, well, when you looked at me you'd relive that moment when you chose my welfare over your baby's."

"Gray, no, losing the baby wasn't your fault."

"You were trying to protect me."

She sighed. "My baby was a blessing, and now she's gone. It isn't your fault or mine. Lee was the bad guy here, remember?"

He nodded.

"Stop it. That's an order," she said. "I know what's going on in that head of yours. Stop blaming yourself for everything. Forgive yourself and love me." She went to him and framed his cheeks with her hands, letting the crutch drop to the porch. "We're not supposed to forget those we've lost, Gray. We're supposed to remember them. You're supposed to remember Hoot and all the wonderful things he taught you. I'm supposed to remember the child that taught me strength. That's how we honor their memories."

"Katie, I—"

She kissed him and it all melted away, the shame, the guilt. Love filled his chest. He pulled her close. He couldn't let this woman go, not now, not ever.

He'd wanted her for so long, since forever. And somehow she was here, making this dream a reality.

She broke the kiss and looked into his eyes. "I'm terribly lost and looking for a guide named Gray Turner."

He pulled her against his chest. "My sweet Katie May. You've found him."

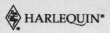

INTRIGUE®

Silhouette®

Desire

NEW YORK TIMES BESTSELLING AUTHOR

DIANA PALMER

A brand-new Long, Tall Texans novel

IRON COWBOY

*Available March 2008
wherever you buy books.*

You can lead a horse to water...

When Alyssa Barkley and Clint Westmoreland
found out that their "fake" marriage was never
rendered void, they are forced to live together
for thirty days. However, Clint loves the single
life and has no intention of being tamed, but
when Alyssa moves in, the sizzling attraction
between them is ignited and neither wants the
thirty days to end.

Look for

TAMING CLINT WESTMORELAND

by

BRENDA JACKSON

Available February wherever you buy books

REQUEST YOUR FREE BOOKS!

**2 FREE NOVELS
PLUS 2
FREE GIFTS!**

HARLEQUIN®

INTRIGUE®

Breathtaking Romantic Suspense

HI07

the DEVIL'S
footprints

**Don't miss
the latest thriller from**

AMANDA
STEVENS

On sale March 2008!

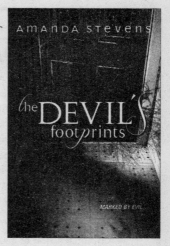

SAVE
$1.00

**off the purchase price of
THE DEVIL'S FOOTPRINTS
by Amanda Stevens.**

Offer valid from March 1, 2008 to May 31, 2008. Redeemable at
participating retail outlets. Limit one coupon per purchase.

52608155

5 65373 00076 2   (8100) 0 11460

® and TM are trademarks owned and used by the trademark owner and/or its licensee.
© 2007 Harlequin Enterprises Limited

MAS2530CPN

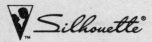

Romantic
SUSPENSE

**Sparked by Danger,
Fueled by Passion.**

When Tech Sergeant Jacob "Mako" Stone opens
his door to a mysterious woman without a past,
he knows his time off is over. As threats to Dee's
life bring her and Jacob together, she must set
aside her pride and accept the help of the military
hero with too many secrets of his own.

Out of Uniform
by Catherine Mann

Available February wherever you buy books.

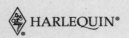